MY KINDA
KINDA
Wedding

USA TODAY BESTSELLING AUTHOR
LACEY BLACK

My Kinda Wedding
A Summer Sisters Novella
Book 7

Copyright © 2018 Lacey Black
Cover Design by Y'all. That Graphic.
Editing by Kara Hildebrand
Format by Integrity Formatting

Published in the United States of America.
All rights reserved.

ISBN-13: 978-1-951829-26-1

MY KINDA
Wedding

Jaime

It's a Summer sister tradition that on the first Saturday of each month, the six of us get together. We take turns picking the location or activity, anything from margaritas and a movie to wine and painting classes at the small gallery uptown. One thing, though, is as certain as the sun rising over the Chesapeake Bay every morning: there will be alcohol involved.

Always.

My husband is late.

Which is why I'm drinking champagne, following my sister Meghan's wedding rehearsal.

This isn't our usual sisters' night. This one is a family-filled event as we prepare to send our final sister off to Marriedland.

After enduring more heartache than I could possibly fathom, Meghan is finally going to have her happily ever after.

More than four years ago, her fiancé was killed in a car accident. It was horrible, not only for her, but for all of us as well. You see, we all loved Josh and were accustomed to having him as part of the family. He fit in so seamlessly, so effortlessly, that we felt his loss immediately, and really, still do today.

But then Nick came along. Sweet, kind, and sexy Nick. He's a badass with a capital B. A dentist by day (and Meggy's boss), and a kids' karate teacher at night. See what I mean? Total badass. And he dotes on my sister. But the best part is that even though he fell in love with her and they're making a life together, he's always accepted her past with Josh and understands that he would always take up just a little bit of real estate in her heart.

That's why I love him.

He's one of the good ones, and the best for my kind-hearted sister, Meghan.

Let's run through the family tree, shall we? It's not like I don't have anything else to do – you know, with chasing a toddler around my sister's rehearsal dinner – while my husband finishes up a project that should have been done weeks ago.

I'm not mad.

Anyway...

First, there's Payton. She's the oldest Summer sister. Owner of Blossoms and Blooms in downtown Jupiter Bay, Payton is married to Dean McIntire, a local accountant. (Of course it was her accountant. Sordid scandal, that was.) Dean brought a daughter, Brielle, from a previous relationship into Payton's organized little world. His ex didn't want to be a mom, and since my big sister wanted to be a mom more than anything, she stepped up, adopting my cute little niece and officially making her part of our family. Brielle is nine now, which is hard to believe, and their son Noah is just over a year. Noah comes after years of infertility and struggles with PCOS, or Polycystic Ovarian Syndrome, but there's no doubt he completes their family in the perfect way.

I'm next in line as second oldest. I'm married to Ryan Elson. (You know, the man who is currently MIA from my sister's wedding rehearsal and dinner?) Anyway, we have the most beautiful, perfect little two-year-old. Well, almost two. Amelia may look like her dad, with dark brown hair and eyes, but her attitude is all me. She's a bit sassy, even at such a young age, but still has that sweet and kind side. And she loves her daddy. Even though I'm going to kill him the moment he walks through the door, I still love that man more than life itself.

I work at Addie's Place, a local not-for-profit that helps kids who are less fortunate with after-school care and homework. Basically, we're a safe place for parents to send their kids, and they'll receive a nutritious snack and all of the important socialization that is vital to a young child's wellbeing and development. I love my job, and can even take Amelia with me, when necessary.

Ryan is a contractor who spends his days building new homes and garages, or remodeling existing ones. He's amazingly talented and has a waitlist a mile long. He works hard, but at the end of the day, drops everything to come home to his family. I'm fortunate like that because he lives and breathes his family as much as we do him.

Up next is AJ, or Alison Jane. AJ is a math teacher at the junior high, and is married to a former pro baseball player, Sexy Randall, as his hashtag proclaims. His actual name is Sawyer, but we like to remind him of his Twitter nickname whenever we can. Sawyer played for the Rangers for ten years before sustaining a career-ending injury while on the field. He moved back to his home state of Virginia and met my sister at a bar one night, before he had started his new job as the PE teacher and baseball coach at the junior high. Yep, coworkers. Another sordid story there.

AJ and Sawyer welcomed my newest nephew Nolan a few months ago. He is the perfect blend of his parents with his dad's blue eyes and my sister's striking features. These two definitely know how to make beautiful babies.

Meghan is fourth in line. I already mentioned what led us to tonight, but I think it's important to reiterate that this relationship has been amazing to watch. What started out as friends and coworkers blossomed into a lifelong love. It wasn't an easy road for them, but together, they powered through. He helped her heal, for that I'm certain, in a way that no one else could. I've been looking forward to tomorrow's nuptials for the last ten months.

Rounding out the Summer clan are the twins Abigail and Alexis. They are as different as night and day, both in personality and appearance. Abby was born just minutes before Lexi, and while they're incredibly close, they couldn't be more dissimilar.

Abby married her best friend, Levi Morgan, a little over a year ago. They live in a great little subdivision with the big fenced-in backyard and the wraparound porch. It's perfect for any future little Morgans they plan to add to their family. Right now, they're happy with a German Sheppard named Riggs. Abby spends her days behind her computer screen, editing books for the romance division of a New York publishing company, while Levi works for the local hospital as an EMT, as well as a volunteer firefighter.

Lexi finishes off the six Summer sisters as the most vocal and most fertile of us all. She works uptown as a hairdresser during the day, but works harder at home taking care of her three kids at night. Lexi and her husband Linkin have twenty-month old twin boys, Hudson and Hemi, and an eleven-month old daughter, Stella, who just so happens to be the same age as my daughter. They were actually born just hours apart, and even though I went into labor first, Stella is a few hours older. Linkin is the lead mechanic at a local repair shop that specializes in classic cars, and together, they are a duo made in baby-making heaven.

We live in Jupiter Bay, Virginia with eight thousand other nosy neighbors who know everyone and everything. From Memorial Day to Labor Day, our coastal town grows dramatically with the summer travel season. Small seaside shops, quaint bed and breakfasts, lots of access to the beach, and local bars and eateries make it a great place to get away for an extended weekend or for some fun in the sun on a holiday.

Our father, Brian Summer, has been the glue that holds our family together for years. We were young girls when our mother, Trisha, lost her fight with ovarian cancer, and ever since then, he's been one of the constants in our lives, trying to make sure six girls all flourished and were cared for. That's also where our grandparents, Orval and Emma, come in.

My dad realized right away that he would need help, raising six daughters and working full time to support us, so he moved our mom's parents in. What I don't think he was prepared for was their constant PDA and grope-fests that resulted in always making sure you knocked before entering any room or knowing more details about the birds and the bees than our health teacher.

Dad has been dating a wonderful woman (also widowed), Cindy Jones. She recently moved in with Dad, which was a big step for all of us. Not because we don't love her – because we do. Dad has been single for so long that it just took a bit of getting used to seeing him with Cindy. Watching them interact, though, is that subtle and beautiful reminder that life does go on.

Tonight and tomorrow's festivities are a testament to that.

"So where's Ryan?" AJ asks as she comes to stand beside me, her son cradled in her arms.

"Your house," I grumble, taking a drink of my champagne and glancing around the room until I find my daughter. She's running around and playing with her many little cousins, my dad hot on their heels to keep them all out of trouble.

"I sense a bit of hostility in your voice. Someone isn't getting road-head tonight," she teases, making me smile.

"Doubtful. Lord knows how long he's going to be working out there. Last I knew he hadn't even painted it yet," I tell my sister, looking toward the door and wishing my husband would walk through it.

Tomorrow, our sister will be married on the beach outside of AJ and Sawyer's home. There's a tent set up in their yard for the post-nuptial celebration, where everyone will enjoy a delicious dinner and dancing. Several dozen chairs will be put out tomorrow morning for the ceremony, in which the happy couple will stand beneath a gorgeous handmade trellis and proclaim their never-ending love for one another.

Except the trellis isn't finished.

Actually, he hadn't even started it until after the rehearsal.

An emergency roofing job ended up taking up all of his time the past two days, which resulted in the one job he had for the wedding not being completed. Now, he's scrambling to get it done – and swears it will be. I know it will be finished and probably more beautiful than anything I could imagine – because that's the type of man he is – but this argument just falls right in line with the one we've had for two weeks.

Don't wait until the last minute to build the trellis.

Exhaling deeply, I turn my thoughts away from my husband and reach for my nephew. Nolan comes easily from his mom's arms to mine and grabs a handful of my long hair. "No, no," I say gently to the little guy in my arms, gingerly pulling the hair from his grip.

"He has a hair fetish," AJ grumbles, taking a drink from her glass.

"Just like his dad," I quip with a knowing smile.

AJ snorts, her eyes seeking out the man in question. She smiles softly the moment she finds him talking with Linkin and Dean across the room. "He comes by it honestly," she says absently.

"Is this little man sleeping any better at night?"

"Not really," she says and yawns, as if on cue. "He still has his nights and days mixed up. Even when we try to keep him awake during the day, he still thinks nighttime is party time."

"That has to be rough," I say, running my finger over my nephew's delicately soft cheeks. He smiles up at me, but I can tell he's getting sleepy.

"It is. Sawyer has been amazing, though. He gets up with me, even though I tell him to get some sleep. We can't both be zombies at school."

"He's a good guy," I assure her, knowing that Sawyer won't be able to just go back to sleep when his wife is up dealing with their wide-awake baby at three a.m.

"He's the best," she coos, glancing his way once more. I look over and watch him crook his finger, indicating he wants her to come to him. She smiles with an ornery glint in her eye, takes their son from my arms, and says, "Excuse me."

I watch as she saunters toward her husband, shaking her hips just a bit more in her stunning purple dress. When she reaches his side, he gazes down at her with so much love and adoration that it makes my heart full. I seriously love the way all of my sisters have found their happily ever after with their soul mates.

Sawyer takes the baby from her arms and gently cradles him against his shoulder. Then, he wraps his arm around his wife's shoulder and pulls her in nice and close.

Yep, he's definitely one of the good ones.

I seek out my daughter again and watch as my niece, Brielle, spins her around on the wooden floor. I can hear Amelia's laughter floating all the way across the room, and my smile is instantaneous. I can't imagine my life without her.

Or Ryan.

Funny, that five years ago, I was moving back home, licking my wounds from my failed engagement. I thought Gavin was my forever, but learned very quickly that I was wrong. Sure, I was devastated when he broke off the engagement, mere days before our big day, but in the grand scheme of things, it was for the best. Without that heartbreaking moment, I wouldn't have met the love of my life.

I wouldn't have Ryan.

Who just so happens to be walking in the door…

Ryan

Adjusting the tie around my neck, I walk through the door of the fancy restaurant, my eyes instantly sweeping the room.

For her.

Jaime.

I spy our daughter, Amelia, first, and smile the moment I see her big toothy grin, as she plays with her cousins. Brielle is there, the oldest of the Summer cousins, and has taken a liking to both Amelia and Stella. I'm glad she has a big family here that she can spend so much time with. My own family is still in New York, but will come down for a visit once or twice a year. We've even made the trip north to see them every Thanksgiving since our daughter was born.

When I see my angel is fine, playing with her cousins, my eyes continue their trek. The room is full of family, but it doesn't take me long to spy my wife. She's standing over by herself, a drink in her hand and those intoxicating green eyes on me. A smile plays on her lips, even though I know she's probably pissed as hell at me.

She told me to work on the trellis many times, but I opted to spend my evenings and weekends with my family. I had set aside yesterday and today to finish up the ornate, handmade trellis that her sister Meghan and fiancé Nick will stand under tomorrow to say 'I do.' Then, work happened. A roofing emergency that required a young family to vacate their home and stay in a hotel, while I had to rip off the entire thing, clear down to the studs in several spots, to repair years worth of dry rot and decay. It was a bitch of a job, keeping me away late last night until after Amelia had fallen sleep, and most of the day today.

Which is why I had to bust ass tonight to make the damn trellis for tomorrow's wedding.

And which is also why I won't complain one bit when my beautiful wife starts her "I told you so's."

She follows my movement as I make my way through the crowd toward her. A few people offer me greetings, but I don't stop to chat. I'm a man on a mission: to kiss my wife.

When she's standing directly in front of me, a smirk on her face that's a cross between I told you so and happy to see me, I wrap my arms around her and pull her into my embrace. She goes willingly, the soft pale blue dress fluttering against my body, and already making me hard. My wife is a fucking knockout, whether she's dressed up or wearing an old t-shirt and shorts around the house.

"So nice of you to show up," she fakes annoyance, though I can see more elation in her eyes than aggravation.

"Well, I had nothing else to do tonight," I reply. "Besides… you."

She blushes in my arms, gripping the back of my dress shirt with one hand. "Did you get it finished?"

"The last coat of paint is drying now," I reply, taking her glass in my hand and bringing it to my lips. When the cool champagne hits my throat, I grimace. "That's not beer."

"No, it isn't."

"That's okay," I reply, setting the glass down on the table beside us. "I don't mind the taste of it… when it's on your lips."

Then I move, kissing my wife for the first time since I left for work very early this morning. She tastes sweet, like champagne and fruit, and like Jaime, a flavor I could never get enough of. My tongue teases her lips, begging for entrance, which she obliges immediately. I don't even care that I'm probably smearing some sort of lip shit all over my face. I'll wear that shade of pink proudly.

"How was our angel tonight?" I ask, nipping at her bottom lip and threading my hands into her hair.

"She was perfect," she replies, breathlessly.

"Let's have another one." The statement doesn't surprise me as it rolls off my tongue. It's not something we've discussed much, but definitely something I've been thinking about a lot lately. I want Amelia to have siblings. Lots of them.

"Usually that doesn't happen right away. They have to cook for, say, nine months," she quips with a smile against my lips.

"I know, but I'm ready for another. Amelia needs a baby brother or sister," I tell her honestly.

"She does," Jaime agrees, hugging me tighter. "She'll make a great big sister."

"The best."

"The closet's available, if you're looking to get a jump start on this plan," I hear in a frail voice just over my shoulder. I can't help but laugh when our private little moment is broken by her grandparents.

"And you know this how?" I ask. The words are out of my mouth before I can reel them back in.

"Weddings make me horny," Emma says with a casual shoulder shrug, while Orval just grins.

"TMI, Grandma," Jaime mumbles, reaching for her champagne glass and finding it empty.

Taking the glass from my wife, I say, "I'll go get you a refill." As I walk away, I can't help but smile as Jaime's eighty-something year old grandma begins to discuss positions for optimal baby making. Silly woman, I'm pretty sure my wife and I have all of those positions down pat by now.

I make my way to the bar and order a refill for Jaime and a Bud Light for myself.

"'Bout time you showed up," my brother-in-law, Linkin, says as he saddles up next to me at the bar.

"Not you too. I've been hearing about it all day via text from my wife. I could practically hear her dramatic sighs of annoyance all the way across town," I tell him with a smile as I pop a bar mint into my mouth. I'm fucking starving.

Linkin laughs. "Oh, I'm sure. If I were in your shoes, Firecracker would have chewed my ass up one side and down the other. She's feisty like that," he says with a smirk.

"I'm not sure I need to hear any more about your wife eating your ass, dude," I tease, earning a laugh from Linkin.

"Look who finally decided to show," Levi says as he joins us at the bar.

"Well, I had nothing better to do," I reply, taking a drink of the beer that's placed in front of me. I throw a few bills on the bar and turn to face the guys.

"I bet. Get everything all wrapped up?" Levi asks.

"Yep. The Sloan family is back in their house tonight and the trellis is on the beach, ready for tomorrow."

"Good deal. I'm sure your wife is breathing a sigh of relief," Levi adds.

"She is thankful I'm finished," I reply, glancing over his shoulder. Jaime walks toward our daughter, who jumps in her mom's arms willingly. Jaime spins her around, both of their dresses flaring out dramatically. I can hear their laughter from over here.

"Excuse me," I say to the guys, patting Linkin on the back as I make my way to my family. They draw me in, like some invisible cord is pulling me in their direction.

I'm already smiling as I approach. "Look how beautiful you are in your dress," I say to my almost-two-year-old daughter, as I place a kiss on her forehead.

"Mommy curled me," she exclaims, grabbing her short brown hair and trying to show me her curls.

"And they look simply stunning," I say with a soft smile, my arms instantly going around my wife. "Are you having fun playing with your cousins?" I ask, resting my chin on Jaime's shoulder.

"Yep! Morrow I play too!" she boasts with a lopsided grin.

"Yes, tomorrow you're going home with Grandpa Brian and Cindy with all of your cousins," Jaime says softly, mimicking our daughter's excitement.

"I can't believe they're taking them all," I whisper.

"Me either. Seven is a lot to handle," my wife replies, her voice tinged with worry.

"They'll be fine. Between the two of them, they raised eight kids," I remind her.

"I know, but it's the first time they've taken them all together."

"The kids will have a blast."

Jaime relaxes in my arms. "You're right, they will."

I nip at her earlobe, running my tongue along the shell. "And we get a whole night of baby making."

Her breath hitches and I feel her sway back into my chest. "We do," she replies in a whisper. She turns her head and places her lips on my own, a gentle kiss that's full of so much promise. It takes all I have not to spin her in my arms and kiss the hell out of her that much more. The only thing that keeps me from doing it is the slap I receive on my cheek and the little giggle that follows.

Before I can remove my lips from my wife's, I feel Amelia's mouth on my chin, giving me kisses too.

Wrapping them tightly in my arms, I can't help but sigh. Damn, I have a good life. A job I love, a beautiful home filled with laughter, a family that I love more than life itself, and a sexy wife who still makes my blood boil with the slightest crook of her finger.

And this is only the beginning…

3

Payton

"Do you think he finished?" I ask my husband, turning my eyes away from where my brother-in-law, Ryan, wraps his arms around my sister.

"I'm sure he did," Dean says beside me, trying to hold on to a wiggly Noah. Our son just wants to get down and run with the rest of them. "He's good at what he does," he reassures me. You'd think it was my wedding day tomorrow, since I've been more stressed about the trellis not being complete than the bride herself.

"You're right, he is. I'm sure it's the best trellis out there."

I glance around at the room, taking in my family mixed with Nick's. Brielle plays with her twin cousins, Hudson and Hemi, while little Stella runs over and steals a bite of something sweet off her mom's fork.

"Do you wish we would have done this?" Dean asks, finally getting Noah to calm down in his arms. Our son is terrible at falling asleep, especially when he thinks he might miss something that's happening around him.

"What?" I ask, slightly confused by his question.

"This. A real wedding."

Glancing over at my husband, I see his concern written all over his handsome face. My mind flashes to our quickie wedding in Las Vegas. The jet ride from my dad, the securing of the marriage license and rings, the ceremony at that beautiful little chapel on the strip.

The reason for the urgency.

My eyes instantly go to my daughter once more. No, she may not be mine by blood, but she's mine in every way that matters. For four years, I've been the only mother she's had – except for Dean's mom, Gretchen. Bri's birth mom took off shortly after she was born, realizing she didn't want the life in front of her. Brielle was this beautiful five-year-old little girl when I met her, and she instantly stole my heart.

When we checked into adoption, it was noted that our relationship was strong, but we lacked the rings on our fingers that a judge would appreciate. With a court date looming to make the adoption final (with no contest from her birth mother), we hopped on a private jet and flew to Vegas.

Best decision I ever made.

"Never," I tell him honestly, stepping into his personal space. He wraps his free arm around my shoulder and pulls me close into his side. Our son is snuggled into the other shoulder, gently mimicking the motions of sucking on a pacifier (which we took away from him two weeks ago), his eyes closed as he drifts off to sleep.

"Are you sure? We could always have a real wedding," he suggests softly.

"We had a real wedding," I remind him. "We just did it differently than most. I loved our intimate little ceremony. I wouldn't change it for anything," I reassure him.

Dean looks at me. "It was pretty special, wasn't it?" He offers me a small grin, his glasses perched on his nose, which somehow makes him that much hotter. He's a serious DILF. You know – Dad I'd Like to Fuck? He knows exactly how much I love those damn glasses.

"What are you thinking about? You just got this look in your eyes like you're ready to pounce on me," he says, his own brown ones heating up a few thousand degrees.

"You. And your glasses. And how much I like it when you take them off right before you come to bed. Naked."

Dean groans quietly beside me. "You have to do that now? Not only am I holding our son, but we're surrounded by family. And I now have a massive hard-on because all I can think about is taking you home and devouring your gorgeous body from head to toe."

"Sign me up," I whisper with a wink, earning me another moan.

"Dean McIntire, did you smuggle a baseball bat into this rehearsal dinner?" Grandma asks as she approaches us.

Now it's my turn to groan. "Don't talk like that around my son," I chastise my grandmother, hoping to spare my poor child's ears of what I had to listen to much of my adult life – and much of my teenage years.

"He'll want to know where he came from, Payters," she coos, reaching over and running a delicate hand over Noah's forehead.

"Yes, but not for another twelve years," Dean adds softly.

"I'll be long gone by then, but I'll be sure to will my magazines and movies to the boy," my grandpa adds, an ornery grin on his face.

"Not necessary, Grandpa," I tell him, trying not to laugh.

"Who else will I leave it all to? Them's my boys!" Grandpa boasts like a proud peacock, making Noah stir in Dean's arms.

"Anyway, I just thought I'd mention that the supply closet is open back by the restrooms. I might have told Ryan and Jaimers already, but they're still up here. So it's free!" Grandma exclaims proudly.

"Grandma, we're not sneaking off to a closet. We're in the middle of Meghan and Nick's rehearsal dinner," I remind the ornery ol' woman.

"I know very well where we are, Payton McIntire. Give me the baby, and go forricate in the closet. Don't you know the bridesmaids are always hooking up at weddings? It's practically a law!" she bellows, drawing the attention of Nick's mom.

"You're incorrigible."

"Yeah, well, you're stubborn," she argues.

"I'm stubborn? You're just still bitter that you lost your red room," I tease.

"I miss that room," Grandpa says softly, placing his hand over his heart.

"Dad needed it for his grandkids," I add.

"Yes, well, I guess it was time to retire the toy room. Your grandpa's hips aren't what they used to be, you know. After the replacement surgery at the end of last year, I knew it was time to let it go," she says, turning to my grandpa. "We have a lot of great memories of that room," she adds, patting his arm gently.

"The best, Emmie," Grandpa replies with a knowing smile.

"Anyway, let's talk about the closet," she says, but I stop her right there.

"We're going to be heading out soon to put Noah to bed. Why don't you find Abby? I bet she'd love to fornicate in a closet," I say of one of my youngest sisters.

"Again, Payton. She'd love to fornicate in a closet *again*."

I pull a grimace, not really wanting to think about my sister doing the nasty in a closet. They're dark and dirty and… well, a freaking closet.

"We'll just go find Abbers and the sexy fireman," Grandma says, grabbing Grandpa by the hand and pulling him toward their next victim.

"Can we not have just one nice family function without the words orgasm or fornication?" I ask, dumbfounded, as they walk away.

"I don't recall them using orgasm, sweetheart," Dean says, gently swaying as he rocks our son.

"No, but it was next. They would have gone into great detail on something I – and no one in this room – wants to know anything about. They're eighty-five, Dean. How in the hell can they still be going strong like rabbits at that age?"

"I think they are the youngest eighty-five-year-olds in the world, and who knows, maybe all of *the sex* keeps them young," he says, wiggling his eyebrows.

I snort. "You said *the sex*."

"I guess they've rubbed off on me in the last few years," he says with a shrug.

"That's not a good thing," I argue, rubbing my son's back as he snoozes against his father's chest.

The sight of these two together still pulls at my heart. There was a time where I thought I'd never have this. In fact, the doctors told me it was almost certain that I wouldn't. I tried to push Dean away, but he wouldn't go. He fought me, tooth and nail, and refused to let me ruin the best thing that ever happened to me.

Dean. Brielle.

And eventually, our Noah.

It's funny that we tried all sorts of things, and nothing worked. The stress of wanting a baby so badly, and not being able to actually conceive, is almost overwhelming. On everyone involved. We decided to take a step back and breathe. Hell, we needed it. You know, decide what steps we might want to take after, and the next thing I know, I'm pregnant. On my own. Without drugs or medicine or crazy books with old wives' tales. Just me and Dean and the beautiful miracle we created.

Our son.

The perfect addition to round out our family...

4

Dean

"He's probably out for the night," I whisper to the beautiful woman standing beside me.

"Yeah, we should head out. We've got a big day tomorrow and could all use a little sleep," she says quietly as she gently rubs our son's back.

Our son.

Something I thought I'd never actually say.

And do you know what? That would have been okay. If I'd spent the rest of my life with only Brielle and Payton, I would have died a happy man. But now that we have Noah? Now I know what it feels like to have a full, happy life. I've got all I need right here, in this room.

"You're probably right," I say, glancing around the room to find our daughter. "You'll have to be the one to round up Miss Bossy Pants."

Payton smiles. "She's been extra bossy tonight with all of her little cousins."

"And she gets it honestly from her mother," I tease, knowing full well that Payton can't argue with me. She'll try, of course, but she knows just as well as everyone else in this room that Payton has always had the mother hen gene down pat, and thoroughly enjoys her role as oldest sister.

She turns my way, her eyebrows pulling together. "Do you want to have sex later?"

"Always."

"Then you have to be nice to me. I can't help it that I'm more authoritative than others," she defends with her hands on her hips. Those damn hips that I love to grab, really dig my fingers into, while I'm buried deep inside her.

"That's a very nice way to put it," I tease with a snort, moving forward and placing a chaste kiss on her lips before she has a chance to argue. "And yes, I'd love some sex later. It's always on the menu."

"Not always," she sasses before turning and heading in the direction of our daughter. I know she's referring to the time I went out with the guys and had a bit too much to drink. I tried to sex it up with my beautiful wife when I got home, but she wasn't too happy with my sloppy drunk state. There was definitely no sex that night.

I watch as she approaches our daughter, attempting to convince her it's time to go. Bri glances at me, clearly not happy about the situation, but heads my way anyhow, shoulders dropped and a clear pout in full swing.

"But, Daddy, I'm not ready to go!" she says quietly the moment she gets close to me as to not wake her baby brother.

"I know, sweetheart, but Noah needs to get to bed, and you have a big day tomorrow as flower girl," I remind my daughter.

"I can't wait!" she proclaims, her brown eyes sparkling under the dim lights.

"Well, let's get home so we can go to bed. The sooner we go to bed, the sooner you wake up and get to be flower girl," Payton says with a smile. Their bond still makes my heart soar, in a very manly way, of course.

"And Aunt Lexi can do my hair?" she asks with excitement.

"Yes," Payton replies.

"And I get to wear my pretty white dress like Aunt Meggy's?" she asks for probably the fiftieth time in the last few days.

"Yes!" Payton exclaims with a laugh. "Let's go say goodnight to Grandpa and Cindy, and we'll get your brother home and in his crib."

They go off together, hand in hand, in the direction of Brian and Cindy. My eyes do what they always do – follow their movements.

"Heading out?" Levi asks in a hushed tone as he comes to stand beside me. He instantly reaches out and rubs Noah's back.

"Yeah, as soon as the girls go say goodbye." I watch as he continues to run a soothing hand down my son's sleeping form, a tiny smile playing on the corner of his lips. "You guys need to have one of these," I add.

Levi's eyes meet mine. "Soon." He glances down at Noah again. "I'm ready."

"Yeah?" I ask, happy for my brother-in-law and sister-in-law. They'd both make great parents.

"Yeah, we've talked about it a bit lately. We just got married last year, and we're enjoying the hell out of the honeymoon phase," he quips with a smirk, making me laugh.

"I recall that phase well."

"You guys gonna have another? Noah needs a little brother or sister," he says innocently, but the question still makes my chest tighten. Everyone knows how difficult it was for us to get pregnant, and I'm just not sure it's worth going through all of that heartache and heavy emotion again.

"Honestly, I'm not sure. If I never see tears on my wife's face from a negative pregnancy test again, that'd be just fine by me."

Levi sobers. "I'm sorry, I wasn't thinking."

"It's okay. I think our family is pretty great as is. If it happens, fine, but I don't think we'll try again like before."

"I don't blame you. Just the thought of Abby being upset makes me want to cut out my heart," Levi says, his eyes seeking out his wife. She's over with Payton now, giving hugs to Brielle and telling her goodnight.

The trio heads our way, Payton offering farewell greetings as they return to where Levi and I are standing. I throw a wave at Brian and Cindy, then grab the diaper bag, pulling it over the shoulder that isn't occupied by a sleeping baby. By the time my wife and daughter return to my side, I have all of our stuff gathered up.

"Ready?" I ask the beautiful woman standing beside me.

"Yes."

"I'm not," Brielle grumbles, clearly not happy that she has to leave the party.

"You'll see everyone tomorrow. It's a big day," Payton reminds our daughter.

"I know," she sighs, heading toward the door.

"Hey, I'll see you at lunch tomorrow. I'm having pizza delivered to the salon," Abby says, her eyes wide with excitement.

"With extra mushroom?" Brielle asks her aunt.

"You know it," she whispers conspiratorially.

"Excellent!" Bri exclaims as we exit the small room in the back of the restaurant where tonight's rehearsal dinner was held.

"Good night," I say to Levi and Abby.

Outside, the early May air is cool as we head to my wife's small SUV. I get Noah strapped into his car seat, while Payton loads up the back with all of our stuff. It's a short drive to our home, but that doesn't stop our daughter from filling every second of it with chatter. A couple of times, I glance over and find Payton just staring out into the dark night, a smile on her lips as she gives the appropriate 'uh huh's' and 'of course's' to Brielle. She's so amazing with her, patient and kind. Even now, at nine years old, when everything is a bit more dramatic than ever before.

When we arrive home, we go about our nightly routine. Payton gets a bottle for Noah, while I help make sure Brielle gets on her pajamas, brushes her teeth, and climbs into bed, without sneaking a package of crackers under the blankets.

Has happened.

Bri's eyelids start to get heavy the moment her head hits the pillow, and I know it won't be long before she's out. It was a big day for everyone, especially her. She takes her flower girl duties very seriously, and made sure to listen to everything Meghan said during the rehearsal.

I can't wait to see her in her dress tomorrow.

And her mother.

Which reminds me, it's time to go find my lovely wife.

We meet in the hallway, as if by some sort of kismet. She gives me the sexiest little grin, one that I know means we're all alone and she has an idea of how to take advantage of this moment. Funny, I have an idea too and it involves throwing that red dress she's wearing on the floor.

"Is she out?" she asks, slowly making her way to me.

"The moment her head hit the pillow," I tell her, wrapping my hand around her hip and pulling her into my arms.

"Noah too. It was a big night," she says, already slightly breathless. The sound makes me want to kiss her.

Soundly.

I waste no time in doing just that. I pin her against the wall, her head knocking into one of the family portraits we took at Christmas. Her hands grip my shirt at my hips as my lips devour hers, hungrily. This kiss is a prelude, a tease for what comes next.

"Come to bed with me, beautiful," I whisper, nipping at her swollen, wet bottom lip.

"There's no place I'd rather be…"

5

Abby

Levi and I help gather dirty plates and silverware, disposing of them in the plastic tub by the kitchen door, while AJ and Sawyer straighten chairs and tables. Nick's parents covered tonight's dinner, even though Nick and Meghan balked about it. They wanted to do it all themselves, but couldn't turn down the offer when his mom pulled out her puppy-dog eyes.

"I think that about covers it," I say to my sister, making sure we leave the room in the back of the restaurant the best we can.

"Looks good to me. The manager said they'll collect the linens after we're gone," AJ chimes in, with one final glance around.

"I say we hit it," says my husband of a year.

It's still so weird to say that word. Husband. It wasn't that long ago that he was merely my friend. My best friend, actually. The one I secretly watched from afar, waiting until my stupid crush was over. Fortunately, it never ended. In fact, it only intensified, and the best part was his feelings did too. We went from friends to lovers in a matter of weeks, and we never looked back.

Oh, it wasn't all wine and roses, though. I mean, men are stupid, so of course, he almost messed it up. We were able to work out his blunder, and it was the best decision I ever made.

Well, besides saying yes to a certain question he popped, while down on one knee.

Glancing his way, I see that twinkle in his hazel eyes that lets me know he's probably thinking something dirty. The man's mind is always in the gutter, but that's okay. I usually benefit greatly from his naughty thoughts. Between that wicked tongue and the apa piercing, I'm a very well satisfied woman.

And often…

"Are you okay? You're all flushed," AJ says, a look of concern mixed with her grin.

"Oh, yeah. Fine," I reply, looking around the room once more to conceal my burning face.

I feel his presence before he wraps his arms around me, pressing his front to my back. He's already hard, which doesn't surprise me. The man is a walking hard-on anytime I'm in the room. "What are you thinking about, Mrs. Morgan?" he whispers in my ear, his warm breath tickling my earlobe.

"Nothing," I reply, and even to my own ear, it comes out all breathy.

"Mmhmmm, nothing. I bet it definitely is *something*," he says quietly, flexing his hips discretely and sliding his cock against my rear.

"Well, maybe it is *something*."

"We should go. Then I'll be able to do *something* about it."

"Are you two talking about sex? Abby has a look on her face like she's about drop to her knees and worship at the altar of Levi," AJ says loudly, drawing the attention of the staff milling about and cleaning up the room.

Again, cue the blush.

"Stop it, Grandma," I tell my older sister.

"Did someone say sex?" Sawyer says, joining our group with a sleeping baby boy on his shoulder.

"He finally fell asleep?" she asks, checking on her infant son, sleeping in his father's arms.

"Finally. If we hurry home, we can get about an hour of Mommy and Daddy alone time before his next feeding," Sawyer adds, wiggling his eyebrows suggestively at my sister.

"You know damn well that the moment we lie him down on his mattress, he's going to be wide awake again," she grumbles, holding in a yawn.

"Then maybe we should drive around for a bit. You know, check out the local parking spots…" he suggests.

"We're not parking with our son, Randall. You'll just have to keep it in your pants until we're home and he's passed out again," AJ says.

"Is he sleeping better yet?" I ask.

"Nope. He's wide awake at night. There isn't enough coffee in the world to help us get through the day, some days," she replies.

"I fell asleep last week at my desk before baseball practice. I had to pretend to be looking over the opponent's roster to cover up the fact that my starting pitcher just busted me sawing logs at school," Sawyer adds.

"I'm sorry," I say to no one in particular. I take a few steps forward to where my sleeping nephew rests, his tiny little mouth gaping open in a deep slumber. "He seems to be out pretty good. Maybe you'll be able to get some sleep," I add in a hushed whisper.

"Don't let the stinker fool you, Abby. He's a pro at taking a power nap so he's raring to go come midnight," AJ adds, covering another yawn.

"Let's get out of here," Levi says, placing a hand on my back and leading me to our table to gather our belongings.

Sawyer gently places their son in his carrier, while AJ makes sure she has bottles, burp rags, and his soft little toys picked up. Levi grabs my clutch purse before I have a chance to pick it up, which makes me grin.

"What?"

"Red is definitely your color," I tease.

"Abby is my color," he replies with a smirk, making my cheeks burn with his innuendo.

Nolan begins to fuss from his seat, his little arms starting to flail and his mouth opening wide, like he's ready to let out a loud wail. Levi turns around quickly, grabs the pacifier in the seat beside the baby, and gently places it in his mouth. My nephew instantly starts sucking hard, calming himself down until he settles back to sleep. The entire time, Levi stays right there, Sawyer standing by his side, as they watch over the infant.

"There's nothing sexier than watching two hot guys dote over a baby," AJ murmurs beside me.

"No kidding," I reply without taking my eyes off my husband.

Some day, he's going to make an amazing dad. He loves spending time with each of my nieces and nephews, even holding them when they were tiny babies. He's gentle, caring, and patient, and my sister's one hundred percent right – it's sexy as hell.

"Time to have one?" she asks quietly, as to not draw attention from the two alphas, protectively watching over the sleeping baby.

"We've talked about it," I confess. "We both want kids."

"No time like the present," AJ says with a grin. "He'll be the best dad," she adds, nodding toward my husband. Levi is softly rubbing Nolan's foot, adoringly gazing down at the sleeper, and quietly chats with Sawyer.

"He will." My heart starts to pound in my chest. We've talked about it, sure, but I'm not sure we're there. Okay, so I'm not sure Levi's there. I'm ready. I've always wanted kids some day, and now that I'm spending those days with Levi, it makes me yearn for one that much more. He really will be the best dad ever, and I can't wait to share that with him.

"Ready?" Levi asks, approaching with a smile.

"Yep," I reply, following my sister and her husband out the door. "Good night," I say, one more time, as we reach their car and they go about securing their son in the back seat.

"See you at the salon," AJ says with a wave.

I can't believe Meghan is getting married. Finally. It's been a long time coming. While we all grieved Josh's death, no one hurt more than my sister, Meghan. It was excruciating to watch, especially when all of us were finding our bit of happiness.

And then Nick came along and showed her how to feel again.

It makes my heart sing with happiness.

"What's wrong?" Levi asks, pulling me into his arms, placing his thumb and pointer finger under my chin, and tilting it upward. He has always been so in tune to me.

"I'm just happy. For Meghan and Nick," I tell him, placing my cheek against his chest.

"Me too," he says, kissing the top of my head and escorting me the rest of the way to his truck.

The ride to our place is quiet, but we've discovered over the last several years, we don't need to fill it with chitchat. Our hands are entwined on the seat between us as a country love ballad plays on the radio. I hum along to the tune, and it doesn't take long for Levi to join in. Only, he sings.

And it never fails that every time he opens his mouth to sing, my panties are ruined.

"What's going on over there," he asks, glancing my way for a second before returning his eyes to the road.

"I was just enjoying listening to you sing."

His eyes darken as he looks my way one more time. He knows the impact his singing has on my body. "I'm not the only one who'll be singing when we get home…"

My body ignites, my blood boils as it zips through my veins. I never knew this sort of reaction was actually possible, outside of reading about it in the romance novels I edit, but ever since my relationship with Levi went to the next level, I feel this burn, this yearn for him twenty-four seven. If someone would have asked me about it years ago, I would have said it was a myth, a fable created by women with nothing better to do than dream up fictional men who don't exist.

But now I know. Now I feel it.

Every day, when I'm with Levi.

I feel it in my heart and soul. I feel it in the way he touches me, looks at me with love and compassion in his eyes, and says all of the things I've always dreamed of hearing. But he's not just saying them to speak – he means them. We're in this together, through thick and thin, and there's no one else I'd rather be on this journey with. He's my best friend, my great love.

And we're just getting started…

6

Levi

There's nothing better than waking up with my wife in my arms.

My Abby.

I feel her tense, even though she pretends to sleep. I'll let her play her little game, as my hands slowly make their way down her hips, her ass pressed firmly against my cock. The sexiest ass in the world. The only ass I will wake to every morning, for the rest of my life.

And I'm completely, one hundred percent okay with that.

The ass in particular wiggles a bit and presses back against my ready-to-go cock. "Good morning," she whispers, her voice tinged with sleep.

"It could be," I reply huskily, running my lips along her smooth neck.

"I have to meet my sisters at the salon soon," she says, her voice hitching just a bit as I continue a downward trek with my lips.

"We're still considered newlyweds, babe. It's appropriate, and maybe even a bit expected, to be a little late." My mouth slides down her shoulders and my hands squeeze her ass, as I gently maneuver my cock toward her sweet pussy.

"You're such a bad influence on me," she gasps the moment I start to slide in from behind.

"Fuck yes, I am," I grunt, suddenly finding myself balls deep in her warmth. Abby turns her head to look back at me, and I'm just fucking lost. Lost in her body, lost in her desire, lost in her love.

I can't believe I fought this, all those years ago. The attraction, the want, I pushed it all aside out of fear. Too afraid of losing the best thing in my life – my best friend – I fought my feelings for her for too long. Now? She's mine, and I'm hers. She owns my heart, wholly, and I'm more than fine with that.

She's my life.

Continuing to move my hips very slowly, I rain kisses down her neck, shoulders, and upper back. I knew exactly when the head of my cock – or more precisely, my piercing – hits that magical spot inside her. Abby gasps and stills in my arms, which makes me only thrust with a bit more force this next time.

I can feel her starting to shake, so I know she's already getting close. My own body starts to tighten, my moves a bit more jerky and my pace picking up. She shudders as I grind my pelvis against her ass, letting my piercing work its magic and take her there. I hear her gasp a second before I feel her tighten around me. My eyes practically cross as she grips my cock and pulls me into her.

"Fuck," I groan. The base of my spine starts to tingle, and I know I'm about to fucking come.

"Levi!" she gasps, the sound of my name on her lips the sweetest blessing in the world, as she starts to come, pulsing tightly around my cock and finishing me off.

Her name spills from my lips as I release everything I have inside of her. Gasping for sweet oxygen, my lips automatically claim her skin, sliding along her neck and tasting the sweat on her shoulders. "So fucking good," I whisper, wanting to stay buried inside of her forever.

"Mmm," she coos, relaxing in my arms.

"We could take this in the *other* room," I tease, placing another kiss on her exposed skin.

Abby gasps. "We're not supposed to be talking about that."

"You mean the swing?" I know she's starting to blush a brilliant shade of red. "The one your grandparents got us that we use as much as humanly possible?"

"Stop talking about it. You'll get used to saying it and eventually let it slip. Then, we'll never hear the end of it from them," she says sternly, making me grin a mile wide.

"Fine," I grumble, pulling her even tighter into my embrace. "I won't talk about it so I don't accidentally let it slip how much my wife loves to be fucked in a sex swing."

"Levi!" she exclaims, a cross between exasperated and excited as she giggles. I can tell because her pussy tightens around my suddenly hardening cock.

"I love it when you say my name." My lips continue to taste her skin. I can never get enough of savoring her. She purrs and gently rocks her hips back against me. "Do you know what else I think?"

"Hmm?"

"I think you should stop taking your pill," I blurt out, and wonder if I made the right call the moment she tenses in my arms.

"You do?"

Again, with a bit of hip action, I reply, "I do."

"Okay," she whispers, turning and looking at me over her shoulder. My heart practically pounds out of my chest as I gaze down at this incredible, beautiful woman. My wife. The very reason I was put on this earth.

And hopefully soon, mother of my child.

"I really want to have a baby with you," I confess, swiping the dark brown strand of hair from her forehead.

"I really want that too," she says, a gorgeous little smile gracing her plump lips.

Lips that I must claim, right now.

My own mouth is urgent, my tongue sweeping in, possessively. I need to feel her skin completely against mine, and it only takes me a second to move both her and myself until she's underneath me. Her legs instantly wrap around my hips and my cock finds its happy place once more. She threads her arms around my back, holding on tight, as my mouth takes control of hers. My tongue mimics each thrust of my cock, taking us both higher and higher toward another release.

We're both loud as we let go, coming fiercely and shuddering against each other, skin on skin.

"I love you," she whispers, making my heart sing in my chest.

"I love you more, Abby. And I really do want to start the next phase of our life together."

She smiles up at me, that earth-shaking, heart-pounding kinda smile that I fell so deeply in love with. "Me too."

Abby curls against my body, both of us sweaty and completely sated. As we relax together, I start to hum the sweet melody to our song – the one I've always sang just for her. "Angel Eyes" by Jeff Healey will forever be our anthem, from our decade-plus long friendship to the love and life we now share together. I feel her smile against my arm, and I know I'm right where I'm supposed to be. I've fucked up a lot of shit in my life, but with Abby, I finally got it right.

She's my song.

I know the minute she falls back asleep. Not only does her entire body relax against me, but the cutest little snore fills our bedroom. Glancing at the clock, I decide to let her snooze for a little longer before waking her. We have a bit of time before she has to meet her sisters at the salon and me, the guys at Lucky's. It's a tradition we started a few years back when Ryan and Jaime got married. We'll meet up at the old bar, have some greasy burgers and fries, and play a few games of pool. It's a great way to relax before we have to don our monkey suits and smile for the camera.

As I hold my wife in my arms, I can't help but wonder if maybe we've created a life. No, I know it's probably not likely, considering she hasn't even stopped taking her birth control yet, but a man can hope, ya know? It amazes me how excited I really am now that we've made the decision. I want to have a baby with Abby. I want to watch her grow big and round. I want to see the moment that life comes screaming into this world. But mostly, I want to experience her as a mother. She'll be fucking fantastic, that I'm sure. Just watching her with all of her nieces and nephews is enough of a confirmation, but to watch her hold *our* baby? That's something in itself.

I continue to hold her tight, my thoughts drifting to today's wedding. I'm so damn happy that Meghan and Nick are finally getting married. It's been a long road, especially for Abby's sister. I remember that night well. The night her life came crashing down around her. Every time I think about something like this happening again, my gut burns with anxiety.

If something happened to my Abby, I'd be lost. I'd never be the same. But my biggest fear is something happening to me, and Abby being left behind to pick up the pieces. It almost happened once, years ago, when I responded to a fire that just so happened to be right next to Payton's business. I fell through the flooring with a fellow firefighter, becoming trapped in the basement. It was the longest thirty minutes of my life, while we waited for help to arrive, and the entire time, I thought about her.

I prayed that God not take me away from Abby because I wasn't done yet. I wasn't done loving her.

Now, every time I respond to a fire, it's there – in the back of my mind. I do everything I can to ensure I return home to the woman I love at the end of my shift, because the thought of leaving her behind to live the way Meghan did for two long years makes me sick to my stomach. There's too much light in her eyes to ever see it dimmed.

Meghan is okay, and today she's marrying the man who she'll spend the rest of her life with. That makes me happy, because even after she walked through so much darkness, she's finally standing on the other side, surrounded by light. And Nick is fucking awesome. He fits into this crazy-ass family well.

Even though I'm not ready, I gently pull my arms from beneath my sleeping wife. After a quick stop in the bathroom to take a leak and throw on a pair of basketball shorts, I'm immediately greeted in the hallway by Riggs, our energetic German Shepherd. He's dancing around in the hall, half with excitement to see me and the other half with the need to pee, and he's hot on my heels as I make my way to the kitchen to start the coffee. Nothing beats the smell of percolating coffee.

Well, maybe Abby…

I check my phone and find a text from Sawyer.

> **Sawyer:** He woke up two minutes after we got home. Thanks for the sleeping vibes, but that shit didn't work. You need to work on your voodoo powers because they suck.

I snort a laugh, recalling how I told him some bullshit last night about sending positive vibes or juju or whatever so that Nolan would sleep a bit when they got home. The man is dying for a little alone time with his wife, if you know what I mean. With a new baby, and the fact that he won't sleep when most of the rest of the East Coast is out, makes getting busy with your wife a difficult task.

> **Me:** Sorry, dude, I tried. Maybe try Benadryl? Linkin is always threatening his twin brothers with that shit when they won't calm down. *insert smirk emoji*

I hit reply, snickering to myself as I pour my first cup of coffee of the morning. No, Linkin has never actually given his brothers Benadryl, but I know he's been frustrated enough to threaten it.

> **Sawyer:** Don't think I haven't thought about it. He's too young, though. Last night, I turned on Sports Center and we watched baseball highlights for an hour while AJ slept.
>
> **Me:** At least one of you caught a bit of shut-eye.
>
> **Sawyer:** Yeah, until I had to wake her up to feed him. The moment I saw him latch on to her tit, I had to excuse myself before I actually became jealous of my three-month-old.
>
> **Me:** *insert laughing gif*

Sawyer:	Laugh it up now, fucker. One of these days, you'll be in the same boat, wishing it was your mouth on those tits and having to go to bed with a hard-on because you're both too damn tired to do anything about it.
Me:	You have tonight. Brian and Cindy are taking all of the kids...
Sawyer:	Is it bad that I'm more excited about getting a night off, alone with my wife, that I don't even care if he keeps everyone else in that house up all night?
Me:	Nope.
Sawyer:	And we'll probably be too damn exhausted to actually do anything.
Me:	*inserts laughing emoji*
Sawyer:	Fucker
Sawyer:	The wife is stirring. I'm going to see if I can catch some action while the house is quiet.

I don't even reply. I hope the guy can get a little before his son wakes up and demands all of their attention.

After setting my phone down, Riggs and I head to our deck to enjoy a cup of coffee. He runs down the stairs to do his business, sniffing out every square inch of his property and inspecting it for intruders. It's still fairly quiet outside, even though it's midmorning. Our neighbors are pretty fucking awesome. They all work regular hours and fill the neighborhood with kids on bicycles and lemonade stands.

Abby and I found this house the day it went on the market. It was an accident, really. We were leaving my chief's house, celebrating the retirement of our captain – a man who had over thirty years with the Jupiter Bay Volunteer Fire Department. We were driving by, enjoying the beautiful, sunny day and admiring the great family homes in the subdivision. Abby saw the house before we were even there, and instantly fell in love with the modern brick exterior and cobblestone walkway.

What caught my attention was the realtor pounding her sign in the front yard. I pulled over immediately, to both Abby's and the real estate agent's surprise. The couple who built the house ten years ago was relocating out of state. They had vacated the property a few weeks before, leaving it for the agency to finish preparing it for sale.

We got lucky that day.

Monica invited us inside for a walk-through, which resulted in a private meeting between my now-wife and I on the back deck. We made an offer, and it was accepted before the sign was fully positioned in the front yard.

Everything happened fast after that. We moved from our tiny little apartment across town and started to fill the new place with furniture with weird names like credenza and dining room buffet. All I cared about was that it was something that made Abby happy, a home we could start making memories in, and maybe fill it with a few kids of our own.

The sliding glass door opens and my eyes are instantly drawn to the woman I love. She's wearing one of my t-shirts – my second favorite thing for her to wear (or not wear) – and has a smile on her face. Riggs sees his mama and quickly bounces up the stairs for a kiss.

"Hey," she says sleepily as she comes over to where I sit.

"Mornin'," I reply, loving how she settles on my lap instead of the seat beside me. "Sleep okay?"

"I got lonely," she answers through a yawn, reaching down and petting our dog. That's one of the only hang-ups with my work schedule. Sometimes, I work nights and Abby always complains that sleeping is impossible without me beside her.

"I'm sorry, sweetheart." I place a kiss on her forehead. "I thought you'd like a bit longer to sleep."

"I did," she says, wrapping her arms around my chest. I pull her tightly against my chest, loving the way the gentle breeze stirs her hair. She smells like vanilla and sunshine. And sex.

"It's almost time to get ready," I tell her, enjoying the quiet of the morning. The birds are chirping and the trees gently swaying. The yard is long, with two huge oak trees that beg for a rope swing and a privacy fence that does nothing to keep the baseballs from flying into our domain.

But nothing beats the feel of this woman in my arms, her gentle breath on my neck. Even with our dog's wet nose draped across her lap, I realize these are the little moments I never want to forget.

"I'm so excited. It's going to be a gorgeous day."

"As long as you're there, my day is perfect." I know, I sound whipped, but it's true.

"I love you," she says softly, her voice that of an angel.

"I love you more, Abby," I reply, turning her just slightly so I can steal another kiss. "Let's go get ready so we can come back here tonight and work on that baby-making thing."

She shivers in my arms, but something tells me it's not entirely from the morning coolness in the air. "I might even suggest a bit of time in the other room," she whispers, a giggle slipping from her lips.

The other room. The swing.

Best idea ever…

7

Lexi

"You were supposed to be here a half hour ago!" I holler at my twin as she steps inside the salon.

"I was... busy," she replies, dropping her shoulders and hiding the blush that's creeping up her cheeks.

"She means they were having *the sex*," Grandma chimes in, drinking something bubbly and yellow from a champagne flute.

"You're drinking already?" Abby asks, setting her purse on the floor and heading in Grandma's direction.

"They're mimosas, Abbers. It's orange juice, which is the perfect brunch beverage. Besides, it would be a sin to let them go to waste," she adds. taking a long drink of her champagne and orange juice mixture.

"I highly doubt you've been repenting for your sins, Grandma," Payton teases from her seat in my chair. Her long brown hair is going up in an elegant, simple twist.

"Oh, I've been talking to God a few times a week, Payters. We might be old, but with the help of modern medicine, everything still works as God intended it to," the oldest woman in the room boasts.

"Gross," Meghan grumbles, chugging a bit of her own drink.

"Take it easy, Meggy Pie. You don't want to be too tipsy when walking down the aisle. You want to keep your wits about you today, so that when you look back years from now, you'll remember every little detail fondly," Grandma says with a smile.

"That's sweet, and you're so right," Meghan replies, setting her flute down.

"And besides, when you go off to engage in *the sex* tonight, you don't want to be throwing up on your man's shoes like AJ," Grandma adds politely, making the entire room crack up.

"That wasn't after our wedding," AJ grumbles.

"No, but it could have been," Grandma replies. "I saw how much you and the ball player were enjoying the open bar at your reception."

"I hope I can remember every detail," Meghan says, a small smile playing on her lips as she sits at Ella's table getting a manicure.

"You will, Meggy," Jaime assures her with a smile. "Today is going to be perfect."

Everyone has been secretly on edge lately, praying that this wedding goes off without a hitch. After everything that

Meghan went through these last few years, no one wants to see anything hinder her big day with Nick. I've watched my sister remain cool and calm as she's prepared and planned this wedding, which really shouldn't surprise me. She's the most levelheaded of all of us Summer girls.

Way more than me.

I'm more of the shoot first, ask questions later kinda girl.

But in my defense, my husband likes to get me all riled up.

Much like he did early this morning… in bed…

Linkin has always had a natural ability to get under my skin, but do you know what? It works for us. He drives me crazy, but then makes up for it with his magical cock. It might be what has kept him alive so damn long. Lord knows I've almost killed him a time or two over the years.

But not really. I'm all talk, in that regard. My husband is the best thing that ever happened to me. He showed up in my life (or, more accurately, on my doorstep) when I needed him the most. Our relationship may have been a bit unconventional in the beginning, you know, with him offering to fertilize my eggs for free, ensuring he be my baby daddy, but it worked for us. *He* works for me, and the thought of not having him beside me in this journey through life is a little scary.

I finish Payton's hair, while Cecelia and Barb work on Jaime, Abby, AJ, Cindy, Grandma, Nick's sister, Natalie, and his mom, Amy. As soon as Payton is done, she heads over to where Noah is playing in a playpen, his little cousins all close by. Yes, the salon is a madhouse right now, but we have my mother-in-law, Karen, and Payton's mother-in-law, Gretchen, as well as Dad's girlfriend, Cindy, all to help keep somewhat order amongst the masses.

"Come on, sweet pea, you're next," I say to my niece, Brielle, who's eyes light up like diamonds the moment I tell her to get in my chair. She's been extremely patient, yet incredibly excited for today's events. She played with all of her little cousins for a while, but she never really took her eyes off my chair.

Brielle hops up in the seat, her smile stretching from ear to ear. When I glance at Meghan, I see the same grin plastered on her face as she looks up at her flower girl.

"I want lots of curls!" Bri exclaims, slightly bouncing as she gazes at me from the mirror.

"Lots and *lots* of curls?" I ask as I pump the chair to raise her up.

"Yes! Lots!" she practically screams, making all of us laugh and smile.

"Inside voice, Brielle," Payton chastises with her own grin, feeding Noah something mushy and smelly from a jar.

"Okay, pretty girl, are you ready?" I ask my niece, pulling her long hair back and running my hands through it.

"Yes," she whispers with excitement.

"This part is uncomfortable for a few minutes, so I'll hurry," I tell her as I help her bend forward, pulling all of her hair so that it's hanging over her face. Then, I start to braid a reverse French braid, starting at the nape of her neck. I work quickly to pull all of her hair into the braid before securing it with a clear rubber band.

When all of her hair is piled on top of her head, I have her sit up. Her face is red from being bent over, but the smile is still there. This girl loves to come to the salon and have her hair messed with. Each time I cut and color her mom's hair, Brielle comes along, playing with the combs and brushes, and sometimes even talking her parents into a strip or two of color.

Grabbing the curling iron, I start to add the curls – lots of them, as per her request – and secure them to her head with a bobby pin. It doesn't take long, and the result is freaking adorable, if I do say so myself. When the curls are all in place, I grab the can of hairspray. "Cover your eyes."

And then I spray her entire head down.

"Ready?" I ask, grabbing the handheld mirror and spinning the chair around.

I hold the mirror so she can see the back of her head in the reflection, and the result is a squeal. "I love it!"

"I think it looks amazing," Meghan gushes as she comes over to stand beside her flower girl.

"Thanks, Aunt Meggy. Mom, do you like it?"

"Oh, that looks phenomenal," Payton adds, a wide smile on her face.

"Can I put on my dress now?" the little girl begs.

"Your dress is at Aunt AJ's house with the rest of them. We'll head over soon and start to get ready," Payton assures her. "Why don't you go have Ella paint your nails," she adds, indicating that it's Bri's turn at the manicure table.

"Yay!" she exclaims as she hops down from my chair before I even have a chance to lower it.

"I think she's excited," Meghan says with a chuckle.

"You think? She's talked of nothing else for weeks. Months, really," Payton says before turning her attention back to Noah.

"You're next," I tell the bride-to-be.

Meghan's eyes light up and she slips onto the chair. Before I can pump her up and grab my cape, my cell phone chimes on my workstation. I glance down to see my husband's name and a photo of him with our daughter Stella light up the screen. "Give me one sec, okay, Meg? I want to make sure everything is all right," I say as I grab my phone and walk toward the back of the shop. I have to step over kids and dodge rolling trucks, but I finally get to the back break room, where it's relatively quiet.

"Hi," I answer in way of greeting.

"Hey, Firecracker, so I was thinking," he starts, the deep purr of his voice instantly warming all of my lady parts.

"About?" I ask, suddenly all breathy.

"We should have another baby."

I blink once, twice, as silence fills the line. I pull my phone away from my head and glance down at the device, wondering if I'm dreaming this entire thing. Nope. There's his name and there's the ticking clock, marking how long our live conversation has lasted so far. "Are you on drugs?"

"Only high on you, baby," he practically growls. Before I can respond, he continues "I was just thinking about how many times you came this morning – you know, twice in bed and once in the shower – and it got me thinking, my wife is a fucking fox anytime, but when she's pregnant? Well, I can't keep my hands off her."

And he keeps talking…

"Plus, when she's pregnant, she pretty much wants my cock twenty-four seven, and let's face it, I'm a huge fan of that. And let's not forget that you're the best mama in the world, and well, I want another baby with you."

My heart is pounding and my breathing shallow. We've talked about this before – and by we've talked about it, *he* has talked about it. I've ignored him. Hell, he was practically talking baby number four the moment I delivered baby number three.

"You're crazy. We're already outnumbered," I remind him.

"I won't be satisfied until we've got a basketball court full," he adds.

"What? I'm not having eleven kids with you!" I practically holler, not even caring that the entire salon – and quite possibly, the entire block – heard.

Linkin chuckles. "Not a football team, Firecracker, a basketball team. Five. We can handle five kids."

"You're crazy," I whisper.

"You've established that. And I'm only crazy for you," he croons, his voice still doing a number on my bits and pieces.

"And we have to decide this now?" I ask, a smile creeping across my lips.

"Now. In fact, if you've got about fifteen minutes, I could be there in three. The guys wouldn't even know I'm gone."

"Not happening, buster. I'm about to work on the bride's hair."

"But this is not off the table, right?"

The eagerness and hopefulness in his voice makes me smile, and before I can really think about what I'm saying, I answer him. "No, it's not off the table."

"Yes! Thank you, baby. I can't wait to make more babies with you," he says softly, the smile in his voice evident.

"You're crazy."

"I know. You tell me often."

"I love you."

"I love you more."

"Doubtful, but can I ask what has gotten into you?" I ask, glancing at the clock and realizing I'm dangerously close to running behind schedule.

"Dean was talking about Noah running in the backyard and slipping in a pile of dog shit, and Sawyer started to say Nolan still isn't sleeping at night."

"Sleepless nights and dog poop do it for you, huh?" I tease.

"*You* do it for me. Stella is almost two. Perfect time to have another."

I sigh deeply, but not because I'm not completely on board with his craziness. In fact, I'm one hundred percent with him. I'd love to have another baby, even though I said Stella was it. Three was our magic number. But here I am, being sweet-talked into more baby-producing sex from my fiend of a husband.

"I really do need to get back in there and start Meghan's hair. Can we talk about this later? After the kids go to my dad's house… and we're all alone… and naked?"

"I'm hard."

"You're always hard."

"True. You make me so fucking hard and crazy."

"My panties are completely ruined," I whisper.

"Fuck, you're so hot I can practically picture you, spread out on the top of our bed. My mouth is watering to taste you."

"Christ, Linkin," I groan, my entire body on fire.

"Put it on speakerphone so I can hear too." Only, this voice isn't coming from the phone. It's coming from behind me, and clearly belongs to someone who is *not* my husband.

"Quit eavesdropping, woman!" I chastise my elderly grandma.

"Emma is there?" Linkin asks, his voice suddenly completely sober.

"I want to hear what he's saying that turns your panties into a useless scrap of material," she coos, her eyes lighting brightly.

"You're incorrigible. Go away," I tell her.

"So you can have more phone sex with the sexy stripper?"

"We're not having phone sex," I defend, my husband's deep chuckle filling the phone, and completely ignoring the stripper bit.

"Were too. I heard you. You were all panting and breathless," Grandma says.

"You were. It was really fucking hot," my husband says via phone.

"Stop encouraging her," I tell him. "I need to go do Meggy's hair so we can finish on schedule. I'll see you later."

"I'll be the sexy fox in the suit who wants to fuck you on the beach later," he croons over the phone line.

"Eww, no. Sand. All over the place. Don't you remember…"

"Oh, I fucking remember. I fucking remember everything, Firecracker."

"I remember digging sand out of places that I never want to again."

"I'll bring a blanket," he adds sweetly. "I love you."

"Love you too," I tell him before hanging up.

"You two are smokin' hot. I'm surprised you're not preggers again," Grandma says.

"We're not trying." Yet.

"Yet," she replies in a singsong voice before turning and walking back into the main part of the salon, humming a happy little tune.

I drop my phone into my pocket, a wicked smile on my face and a shake of my head. I can't believe I just agreed to have another baby. Well, not that it really took much convincing on his part. The thought of expanding our family is both exciting and nerve racking. We really do have everything set up well right now. We have a routine down, a schedule in place, a house the right size, and a system for ensuring the kids don't completely overthrow the household.

Another baby?

With my super sexy husband?

Yeah, sign me up…

8

Linkin

I'm still smiling as I drop my phone into my pocket and head out of the storage room and into the bar. Picking up the phone and calling her was completely on a whim, but I have to admit, I'm a bit ecstatic with the results.

Since the moment I met her, I knew that she'd be my everything. Sure, it was a bit messy at times, especially there in the beginning, but it all worked out as it was supposed to in the end. She's my wife – my life – and has given me three beautiful kids.

Now I want more.

If she would have said no, I'd be okay with that. Of course, I'd take my time trying to convince her later tonight, but at the end of the day, this is her decision. I'd have a dozen if she'd let me, but I know that's not logical. I wasn't kidding when I said a basketball team. Five. Five little kids with her emerald green eyes and firecracker spirit. I'm not sure if we'll get there or not, but I'm sure as hell going to love the fuck out of trying for them.

"Why are you smiling? You get lucky in that closet?" Ryan asks, nursing his beer at the bar.

"Definitely not," I answer, patting him on the back as I sit down. "My wife is occupied at the moment."

"You had phone sex," Orval chimes in from the end of the bar. Everyone looks down at him and then at me.

"Really?" Dean asks, his eyes smiling as wide as his lips.

"Not really, but I did enjoy talking to my wife," I answer before taking a big pull from my beer bottle.

We all sit at the quiet bar on this Saturday afternoon, eating chips and salsa, peanuts, and popcorn. Rhenn, Nick's friend and best man, comes in a few minutes later.

"Sorry I'm late, fellas. I had a prior engagement that needed attending to," he says, a smug smile on his face.

"And by attending to, he means either a barely legal blonde or a recent divorcee," Nick mutters, shaking his head.

"Don't be jealous, Nicky boy. Not my fault you're stuck with the same flavor of ice cream for the rest of your life," Rhenn adds, slapping his friend on the back and giving him a wolfish smile.

"I don't want more flavors. I want Meghan," he replies, earning an agreement from pretty much every guy in the room.

"You boys don't know what you're missing," Rhenn says right before he orders a beer from Lucky.

"I think you don't know what you're missing," I reply. The thought of dating, either casually or otherwise, makes my gut churn.

"I keep telling him that someday he'll get smacked upside the head by the right woman. She won't have triple D's or bleached blonde hair," Nick starts.

"That sounds horrible," Rhenn grumbles, shivering in disgust.

"But she'll have you firmly by the balls. It's coming," Nick says, popping a peanut into his mouth.

"We all fall someday," Sawyer adds.

"Nope. Not me. I'm never falling again," Rhenn says, averting his eyes, but not before I catch something dark and stormy brewing. Something tells me there's a story there and it didn't end so well for him.

"I'm getting hungry," Nick says, pulling the small cardboard menu from the napkin dispenser.

"Me too. Where the hell is Levi?" Dean asks, glancing toward the door.

"He'll be here," my father-in-law says just before the door opens.

"About time you showed up," I holler as Levi steps inside the bar.

"I think he was gettin' some," Ryan adds with a smirk.

"Definitely. There's only one reason a man is late to hang with his buddies, and it isn't because he was stuck in traffic," Dean quips from his seat.

"Leave him alone, guys. He's still in the honeymoon phase," Sawyer defends, popping peanuts into his mouth.

"I can't wait for that phase," Nick says with a smile. "Not that there's any issue with that part now, I mean," he quickly adds.

"It's the best part of getting married," Sawyer agrees, slapping Nick on the back. "Well, besides the actually being married part."

"Truth," I reply to my brothers-in-law and the man who will join the ranks in approximately four hours. "We've got two hours before we have to head back to my place and start getting ready," I add as Lucky comes to take our burger order.

After lunch and a few games of pool, we'll stop by AJ and Sawyer's house to put out the chairs before we all go back to our place to dress in our suits. The girls will all finish getting ready at Sawyer and AJ's house, and if I'm lucky, I'll be able to steal a kiss from my wife before the ceremony starts. It will be on the smaller side, with only about four-dozen chairs being placed on the beach for Nick and Meghan's closest family and friends. It shouldn't take us too long to make sure everything is ready to go.

"You know, back before my Emmie and I got married, we had a pregnancy scare," Orval says, drawing the attention of everyone at the bar.

The room is silent for several seconds as we all wait to find out why he decided to bring this up now. "Really?" Sawyer finally asks, all eyes on the elderly man in the room.

"Yep. It was a few months before we were to be married. After a weekend with Ava and Frank – they got into this huge fight, by the way – well, my Emmie was late on her womanly time. It made the entire trip to Europe very tense."

"Wait, who are Ava and Frank?" I ask, trying to run through a list of family and coming up short.

"Why were you in Europe?" Ryan asks, a questioning look on his face.

"I thought you got married after you left the military?" Dean chimes in.

Orval nods his head. "Just wait, and I'll answer all of your questions. I had just left the service and reconnected with an ol' friend. He was going through a divorce from his wife, Nancy. Frank was in a hurry to marry his Ava, so after his divorce was final, we all hopped on a plane for Paris. We visited Rome, London, and Prague during our two-week stint."

Orval shakes his head as if recalling the trip. "Of course, his production crew was on him to come back for the rest of his shows. Plus, the theater had arranged an Orchestra for a new song they wanted him to cut. Everyone wanted a piece of Frank," Orval says, staring off at nothing.

We're all silent for many heartbeats before Levi finally speaks up. "So… the pregnancy scare?"

"Oh, yes. We had just returned from Europe and Emmie was working with my mother to plan the wedding. Somewhere along the way, she missed her womanly time and we were afraid she was pregnant. That would have been a bit awkward, since premarital sexual intercourse was frowned upon back in the early fifties. But my Emmie was a frisky little thing, and she couldn't keep her hands off my love sword. Who am I to deny?"

"Yeah, that's not surprising, Orval," Nick says with a laugh.

"Anyway, turns out she wasn't pregnant, not that I would have minded."

Again, silence fills the bar. Even Lucky is standing there, listening to the old man's tale of love and life in the early fifties.

"So, then your point was…" I ask, not quite sure where the whole pregnancy thing comes into play here.

"My point is, boys, that sometimes life throws you curve balls and the potential of a surprise baby."

"Who was talking about a surprise baby?" Sawyer asks, glancing around the room.

"No one," Orval answers, taking a drink of his Coke.

Again the room is silent as everyone tries to figure out what just happened. I mean, Orval can be kinda random at times, but this seems a bit odd, even for him. Just blurting out that he and Emma had a pregnancy scare? Suddenly, I'm a bit nervous. Is he talking about someone in this room? Lexi? When was the last time she had her period? I mean, we've been on birth control, but that's not one hundred percent foolproof.

Quickly, I grab my phone from my pocket and fire off a text. It only takes her a few seconds to respond.

Lexi:	What the fuckety fucksticks, Linkin? Are you high? Why are you asking if I've missed my period?
Me:	I'm just checking.
Lexi:	You're so weird.
Me:	So, you haven't missed anything?
Lexi:	Uhhh, no, crazy pants. And you'd be the first to know if I had.
Me:	Ok. Just checking... Love ya.

I set my phone down and see everyone else on theirs too. Levi, Dean, Ryan, and Sawyer are all texting, probably doing the same thing as me. It's just too weird that Orval decided to bring up that story now, especially when no one was talking about surprise babies or pregnancy scares. Though, for me, no pregnancy would be considered a scare. It would be very welcome, actually, and I suspect the same for everyone in this room.

After everyone sets down their phones and glances around the room, Lucky delivers lunch. We all dive into the burgers and fries like we haven't eaten in days. Hell, there must be something about having a baby that brings out the hunger in men. (Not that kinda hunger.) Though, after my phone call earlier to the most beautiful woman in the world, and her confirming we could try for another baby, I'm feeling pretty fucking hungry, if you know what I mean.

Orval sits over on his stool, slowly dipping French fries in ketchup, and without a care in the world. He did that shit on purpose. Got us all riled up. It was probably a bunch of bullshit anyway. No one is late. No one is pregnant (for a change). He's sitting over there, smug as shit, and laughing at all of us. He probably doesn't even have a friend named Frank. Surely not one who was in theater or on television or married to a woman named Ava.

My heart pounds in my chest as I glance over that the ol' kook. A small smile plays on his lips. Frank. Ava.

The. Fuck?

"You knew Frank Sinatra?" I demand from across the bar.

"Ol' Frankie? Of course, I did. We went way back. Talented young man, he was," Orval says softly, smiling wider now than ever before. "Who do you think taught him how to be such a ladies' man?"

This man never ceases to surprise me…

AJ

We're less than two hours out from the wedding.

The guys are out back getting the chairs set up, while Payton and Karen finish the flowers and decorations. Where am I? Stuck in the house, half dressed, feeding my son because he's always hungry. Everyone slipped into their dresses moments before the photographer arrived to take a few pre-wedding pictures. My son, however, decided to wake up from his nice little nap and demand food.

Like always.

I'm tucked away in his bedroom, rocking in the chair my dad bought us for a baby gift. I should be wearing my bridesmaid dress by now, getting ready to take pictures down on the beach with my sisters. Thank God Meghan has been the most laidback bride in history, because the moment my son started crying for food, she just offered me a smile and said, "Go. Pictures can wait."

So here I am, my left breast exposed, while Nolan eats like he hasn't seen food in days. I gaze down lovingly at the little man who completely stole my heart almost four short months ago. He came into this world screaming, his face red in anger and already starving, while his father and I fell helplessly in love with the squishy little child placed in my arms.

Running a finger over his forehead, I watch as he continues to suckle on my left breast, his hand protectively holding the right one as if I could take it away from him at any minute.

Like father, like son

He's definitely a boob man.

I didn't think I wanted to breastfeed. It seems so personal, you know? Not in a bad way, but I didn't want to be one of those women who whips them out everywhere. But the moment I held him to my chest and his tiny mouth latched on like there was no tomorrow? Well, I decided to give it a try, and here we are, nearly four months later and he feeds like a champion. In fact, he's such a good eater that we get to start incorporating some mushy solids after his appointment next week, like peas and green beans.

Continuing to run my finger over his forehead, my eyes watch his every move. He's usually so active, except when he eats. It's like he has one job to do and he does it well. No, he's not too big for his age. In fact, he's only slightly in the seventy-fifth percentile, but this kid takes his food very seriously.

He's so much like his father that it's almost scary. He likes to sit up and watch everything, especially baseball. Do you know how many times I've gotten up in the middle of the night and found my two boys watching highlights on Sports Center? And

Nolan actually watches, as if he's learning the game and dissecting plays.

You're probably wondering about his name, right?

Funny story there.

I told Sawyer that under no circumstances were we naming him a baseball name. No Babe or Ozzie or Jackie or Joe. I wanted a totally normal, non-baseball-y name, like any normal woman. I saw Nolan online and fell in love with it. I remember the day I came home and told my husband. He had just returned from a run on the beach, his sweaty chest on full display and completely distracting, with little beads of sweat falling down his eight-pack abs and toward the happy trail and V of his hips…

See? Completely distracting.

Anyway, he was chugging a bottle of water, knowing full well that I was sitting there, gawking like a perv at his perfection. At eight months pregnant, I could totally blame the objectification on hormones. I mean, he is my husband, and it's not my fault I find him completely sexy and totally fuck-able, even when he's covered in sweat.

So, I was sitting there, staring and completely ignoring the magazine in my hands, when I told him I found the perfect name for our son. He just raised an eyebrow at me, waiting for me to lay my suggestion at his feet and completely fall in love with it.

Nolan.

The perfect name. Not too weird, not too metro, and not too baseball-y.

My sexy husband watched me for a few moments, probably waiting to see if this was a joke. His uber-sexy lips slowly slid upward, his smile completely taking over his face and rendering my not-in-the-least-bit-sexy, almost granny pregnancy panties useless.

"Perfect," he had said.

And it was decided right then and there.

Name on birth certificate.

Nolan Sawyer Randall.

Now, imagine my surprise when we're at home a few days later and Joel flies into town to meet his new pseudo-nephew. Joel is Sawyer's friend and former teammate, and the moment he walked in and saw baby Nolan, he started laughing, complimenting my husband on "winning" the name game.

Excuse me?

I just pushed a watermelon out of my vagina and my husband won the game?

Did you know Nolan *is* actually a baseball name? And not just any baseball name, but *the* baseball name. So it's not *a* baseball-y name, but it's like the biggest baseball-y name in the world of baseball.

Freaking Nolan Ryan.

And freaking Sawyer Randall for just smiling his uber-sexy smile and winning the name game.

Asshole.

Little blue eyes stare up at me, as if he knows I'm thinking smack about his daddy. He's barely eating now, which hopefully means he has filled up his little Buddha belly and is ready to be good for a bit so I can get dressed and on the beach for pictures. But instead of setting him against my shoulder for a burp, I find myself just watching him watch me. This is my favorite part of breastfeeding. Sure, I love that he's getting the proper nutrients needed to grow big and strong, but I love this:

the way he gazes up at me, his blue eyes that are so very much like his dad's, so trusting and full of love.

This little man is my biggest joy and greatest weakness.

I would do anything for him, as would his father.

There's a knock on the door, and I expect it to be one of my sisters. You know, since we're supposed to be on the beach taking pre-wedding photos and all. But the smile that crests my face isn't for one of them. It's for my husband.

He enters slowly, careful not to wake up our son, but he doesn't know that Nolan's a big faker. "How's he doing?" he whispers as he approaches the rocking chair. As soon as our little man hears his dad, his eyes fly across the room until he finds the source of the voice. Sawyer smiles instantly the second his son spots him. "Hey, little man, are you being good for Mommy?"

That's precisely the moment I become chopped liver. Nolan releases his semi-hold on my breast and reaches for his dad. "He hasn't burped," I tell him, adjusting my bra to cover my exposed chest.

Sawyer walks over to the table and grabs the cloth, throwing it over his shoulder as if he's done this a thousand times before (he has), and sets out to get a burp from our son. It doesn't take long, as usual, and Nolan is happy as a clam in his dad's arms.

"How was he?" Sawyer asks, placing a kiss on top of his fuzzy head.

"He was awesome. He was held the entire time and he was doted on by all of the women," I say, referring to the fact that everyone took turns holding the youngest child at the salon earlier.

"That's my boy," Sawyer coos, earning a baby babble and drooly smile from the baby in his arms.

"Did you get everything set up?" I ask, making sure my shirt is righted and stepping into my husband's waiting arm.

"Yep. The chairs are all there. Payton and Karen were wrapping up the flowers and shit. I think they were getting ready to take pictures," he says, his free arm wrapped around my shoulder and pulling me into his embrace.

"I know. They're waiting on me," I say through a yawn.

"Why don't I take him with me?" Sawyer offers. I glance up, lost in those sexy blue eyes of his. "He's already eaten, so he should be good for a while. He can go back to Linkin and Lexi's with me and hang out with the guys for a bit." Gazing down at our son, he says, "You'd like that, right, buddy? Hang out with the guys? Get away from all the girls who just want to kiss your cheeks? That'll be cool in a few years, but now, not so much," Sawyer says with a slight bounce of the arm he's holding Nolan with.

Nolan instantly starts to babble and spit bubbles. "I think he's excited to go hang with the boys," I say as our baby reaches for his dad's stubbly jaw. "I thought you were going to shave," I add, running a finger along the side of his face and instantly feeling the slow burn ignite between my legs.

"I have it on good authority that my wife prefers me a little stubbly. It drives her wild," Sawyer whispers, his eyes locked on mine.

"It does," I answer a bit breathlessly, running a full hand along his jaw. "Completely wild."

His eyes darken to sapphires and I can already tell his pants are getting a bit tight against my hip. It takes every ounce of control I can find not to throw him down on the floor and ride him like a carousel horse. Nice. And. Slow.

"You're thinking something dirty," he whispers, bending down and running his nose along the shell of my ear and inhaling. "I want to do so many fucking dirty things to you."

My panties are useless. My brain isn't working. My lungs practically forget their sole purpose in life. I'm just a panting, wanton woman, wishing her husband would devour her from head to toe. "Yes, please."

"Randall! No fornicating with a bridesmaid before the wedding," Linkin hollers from somewhere deep in the house, making Sawyer groan in frustration. Throw in the fact that our son is trying to push his face between ours, well, let's just say that our private little thirty-second moment was broken.

"I really like fornicating," Sawyer grumbles, adjusting his pants and the baby in his arms.

"I miss fornicating," I add quietly, reaching over and rubbing Nolan's back.

Sawyer pulls me into his arms as best he can while holding a kid, and whispers, "Tonight, you're mine."

I can't even breathe, let alone answer, but the moment doesn't actually require an answer from me. It wasn't a question, but a statement. One that said the moment we're alone, he's going to take great pleasure in doing dirty and very pleasurable things to my body.

I shiver in anticipation.

"Randall!" Linkin hollers, making us both sigh.

"I can't wait," I tell my husband, hugging him tightly.

"It's been so long since I've been inside you, but I promise it'll be the best two minutes of your life," he jokes.

"When have you ever only lasted two minutes?"

"When has it been forever since I've fucked my gorgeous wife? I'm liable to slide inside and embarrass the hell out of myself."

"Doubtful," I say, running a hand up his back and pressing my full breasts against his chest. "And if that's a worry, we might just have to do a little pregame," I add, knowing he's so dangerously close to losing all sense of control.

"I fucking love a good pregame," he tells me, his cock pressed tightly between us.

"Then it's a date. Meet me in the laundry room five minutes after my dad takes all of the kids back to their house," I state, my finger gliding up his chest and toying with his nipple.

"This is our house and I have to meet you in the laundry room?" he asks, his eyebrows pulling upward in question.

"Everyone would expect us to slip off to the bedroom," I reason, placing a kiss on his coarse jaw. "And besides, I really like how convenient it is that the dryer is at perfect level for your mouth and my pussy," I add in a whisper, so only he can hear.

"Fuck, I'm never going to make it through this wedding," he groans, placing a chaste, hard kiss on my lips.

"Randall, dammit!" I hear, moments before heavy footsteps echo hard on the steps.

"You better go before Linkin blows a gasket," I say with a smile.

Sawyer heads to the door and is greeted by Linkin's annoyed face the moment he opens it. "Five hours. You can't wait five damn hours before sexing it up with your wife?"

"Stop being dramatic," Sawyer replies to Lexi's husband. "I wasn't sexing her."

"Yet," I add.

When his blue eyes land on mine, they heat up all over again. "Yet. I was offering to take Nolan with me so she could get ready for pictures," my husband agrees.

"Right, I always take my kid with a hard-on too," Linkin deadpans, an annoyed look on his face. I can't help but glance down and notice Sawyer's slightly tented pants, which makes me laugh.

"I hate you," Sawyer mumbles to the man across from him before turning around and walking toward the dresser. I watch as he throws a couple of things into the diaper bag and grabs the soft blue baseball blanket that Nolan likes to snuggle with.

"You do not. You love me," Linkin sasses, an ornery grin on his smug face.

"Nope," Sawyer replies, turning and giving me a kiss on the lips. "I'll grab a few things from the kitchen and head out. We'll be back right before the ceremony."

"Thank you," I say, feeling slightly relieved that I won't have to figure out how to manage a needy baby and be a bridesmaid and smile for the pictures at the same time.

"Love you," he says before following Linkin out the door, Nolan happily cooing as they head down the hall.

I, on the other hand, do the one thing I shouldn't: sit back down.

I know I should get up and put on my dress. Everyone is waiting on me so we can head down to the beach, but as soon as my butt hits the cushion, my eyes instantly start to droop and the exhaustion that has followed me around for nearly four months starts to pull me under.

I can take a quick little five-minute power nap, right?

I'll just close my eyes for a few seconds...

10

Sawyer

"Five bucks says Mommy lies down and falls asleep, Nolan," I say to my baby boy as I strap him in his carrier. He stares up at me, his eyes wide with excitement, as he babbles his reply to our little conversation.

Linkin comes down the stairs, a boy in each arm. I glance his way, my eyebrows shooting to the ceiling. "Mommy was starting to get stressed out, so the boys are with me," he just confirms what I already suspected.

I make a stop in the kitchen and grab an emergency bottle and formula. I just gotta be careful not to get him too messy right before this wedding, or Mama's gonna be pissed when we get back. Last time I had him solo, I was cleaning dried breast milk and cereal out of his ears for two days.

"Are we ready?" Dean asks when he comes into the living room, his son Noah in his arms.

"We?" I ask, laughing at this turn of events.

"We. Payton can't chase this little one while she's taking pictures, so I'm taking him back to Linkin's place with me. I see I'm not the only one," he says as I pick up our diaper bag and the carrier.

"Nope. Looks like we're all taking a turn," I say as I reach the front door. "You wanna just ride with me?" I ask Dean. I'd offer Linkin, but I don't have enough room for his crew.

"Sure. Let me grab the bag and car seat," he says.

"You guys are still here?" Lexi asks, walking down the stairs with Stella in her arms and her twin sister at her side.

"Heading out now, babe," Linkin answers. "See you in a bit." He kisses his wife soundly on the lips before heading out, his twin boys in his arms.

"The others already take off?" Abby asks, glancing around the room for her husband.

"Yeah, he left with Ryan a few minutes ago," Dean answers just as his wife comes down the stairs.

It's the first time I really notice their dresses. They're long and a shade of purple that looks almost gray in the sunlight. I can't wait to see my wife in hers, though I know she'll be the most stunning woman in the world. Frankly, if I'm being honest, I'm more excited to get her out if it later tonight when we can be alone.

"Is the photographer here? How tight are his pants?" Emma says as she descends the stairs in grand fashion, wearing a light green dress and a wide smile.

"Woman, don't embarrass us," Lexi chastises her elderly grandma.

"Don't sass me, Alexis Renee. When you get to be my age, it's perfectly acceptable to gape at butts," Emma argues.

"Yes, but gaping and grabbing are two totally different things," Abby chimes in.

"Only on the police report, Abs," Emma replies with an ornery grin.

"Good luck with the pictures," I holler to my wife's sisters as I head out the door, Dean and Noah hot on our heels.

It's not a long trip to Linkin and Lexi's place, and Nolan remains awake for the entire ride. He's not used to having entertainment in the form of his cousin sitting next to him, and each time I glance back, I find him completely enthralled with Noah's chatter.

Inside, the house is bursting at the seams. Besides Nick, his dad, brother-in-law, and friend, Rhenn, are there. Throw in Brian, Ryan, Linkin, Dean, Levi, Orval, me, and four little boys, there's definitely some noise in this place. Everyone tries to talk over the person next to them, and the kids start to drag all of the toys out of the playroom and into the main living room. And Nolan? He just takes it all in.

"Hey, buddy," Brian says to Nolan as he comes over to where I stand.

"I'm hoping maybe he'll stay awake a bit so he sleeps tonight for you," I tell my father-in-law honestly.

"Ehh, I'm not worried. If he keeps us up all night, so be it," he replies, taking my son from my arms.

"You say that now, but at three a.m. you may be singing a different tune and calling us to come get him."

"Nah, we'll be fine. Besides, it's one night for us, and one night of sleep for you guys. I remember what it was like to have one that didn't like to sleep at night," he says, tucking his youngest grandson against his chest like a pro.

"Which one?" I ask.

"Do you really need to ask? Where do you think this guy gets it?" Brian says, gazing down at Nolan with a fond smile on his lips.

"I'll admit, I'm really looking forward to catching a bit of sleep tonight," I confess, feeling slightly guilty for saying it aloud.

"Don't be. You're not the first parent in the world willing to trade a kidney for a little shut-eye," he says with a smile.

"Probably not, but I still feel bad pawning him off on you guys before he's sleeping well."

"You didn't pawn him off on us, we offered to take him. And we're happy to do it."

"You and Cindy are a lifesaver," I tell him, and before I can stop myself, I add, "And I'm really looking forward to a little uninterrupted alone time with my wife."

Brian glances at me, his face completely void of emotion. "I'm glad, though if you keep those details to yourself, I'm sure we'll all be better off." I can't help but smile at his slightly uncomfortable face.

"Yeah, that's probably for the best," I reply with a slight chuckle. The things I want to do to his daughter...

We spend the next hour laughing and enjoying a bit of food. Not that any of us are hungry – not after the big burgers and fries we all consumed at Lucky's. I think we're all just anxious for the wedding and doing whatever to keep our hands busy. And later, I can keep my hands busy with my wife...

"How is the school year wrapping up?" Rhenn asks casually, a beer in his hand.

"Good. The baseball team did well," I tell him, recalling how we went to the county tournament and made it to the championship game. We lost, but the guys played their hearts out. I'm definitely proud of the season we had.

"I heard. One of my karate students is on the team. He's always telling me about the games and his awesome coach who used to play in the olden days," Rhenn says, his eyes lighting up with laughter.

"Olden days? Ouch," I reply with a laugh. "It's funny they all recall that I'm a former pro player, but since it happened when they were still in elementary school, it was a lifetime ago to them."

"Only a few years, man, but you better get used to it. I'm approaching mid-thirties, but in their eyes, I was one of the survivors on the Titanic," Rhenn says, shaking his head.

We visit for a bit longer, and I've discovered that Nick's best friend and I actually have a lot in common. He's an electrician by day, and spends his nights at his dojo uptown teaching karate and self-defense classes. His last classes were this past week, so he'll have the summer off to hang out and sail.

"Anytime you want to go out on the boat, just let me know. We could do a guys trip later in the summer," Rhenn offers.

"That sounds great," I tell him, though part of me wants to include my wife. Guys trips are nice and all, but I actually prefer the company of the woman with my last name as opposed to a room full of guys. I did enough of that shit when I was playing ball. Plus, with this group, we all have it bad enough that all we do is sit around and talk about our wives anyway.

"Guys, it's time to start getting ready," Dean announces, his son in his arms. We all glance over to find Nick practically jumping up out of the chair and make a beeline to the room where his suit awaits.

The rest of us decide to take turns getting dressed, so we have a little help with the extra humans we've acquired this afternoon. I'm grateful Nolan is still awake. Maybe he'll nap during the wedding and not give me fits. He might even take just a short nap and be awake for the reception. Then, fingers crossed that he sleeps well for his grandpa later tonight.

Just as I'm ready to take a seat and wait for my cue to throw on my suit, my phone dings a message. I grab it quickly, surprised to see Lexi's name instead of my wife's. When I open the notification, a picture pops up, and I instantly start laughing. There's my wife, wearing the same shirt and stretch pants as earlier, her long hair pinned up on the sides, yet cascading down the long column of her slender neck, and sitting in the rocking chair in Nolan's room. She looks amazing, gorgeous, and frankly just as stunning as the night I met her. She's always been the only woman to completely steal my breath and my sanity, all at the same time. My cock actually starts to perk up a bit, as images of our pending night alone start to play through my mind.

She's also very much asleep…

Meghan

I thought this day would never arrive. I thought any hopes and dreams of a beautiful wedding were crushed the night Josh died.

I was wrong.

As I gaze at my reflection in the mirror, I'm feeling both elation and sadness sweep through me. For so long, I thought this would be my life with Josh. That was quickly replaced by a profound grief that I thought would accompany me through the rest of my days. And then Nick stepped in and showed me that life was worth living. It wasn't easy. In fact, some days I made it damn hard on him, but do you know what? He stuck by me, held my hand, and reassured me that I would be okay.

And I was.

I am.

I miss Josh every day. Every. Day. But when I think back on our short time together, I smile. He was my friend and lover, but not my forever. Yes, it still hurts to say that, and probably always will.

Now I have Nick. A man who gets me, understands my anxiety and pain, and stands beside me with nothing but love and support in his eyes. I can't change the past, but I can embrace the future. My future.

Our future.

This white dress is perfect. Not even close to the one I had my eye on before (you know, when I was planning my first wedding). This one is simpler. It's white with a lace overlay, but with not one ounce of poof. It hugs my curves in a seductive, yet classy way, and I can't wait for Nick to see it.

My hair is pulled back, a long braid-ish style hanging down my back. It's not something I would have picked on my own, but I trusted my sister to come up with a unique style that fit me, and man, did she knock it out of the park. She added a few flowers that Payton brought, and the end result is stunning.

Deep breaths.

"It's time," AJ says at the doorway of her bedroom. She turned over her bedroom for me to finish getting ready, while the rest of my sisters get dressed in the other rooms down the hall.

My sister looks stunning. Her hair is swept back, and the dress fits her perfectly, like the rest of my bridesmaids. All five of my sisters. My best friends. I couldn't imagine this day without them standing by my side.

"Did you have a nice nap?" I ask, grabbing the delicate lace and satin of my dress and hiking it up just a bit so I don't step on the material.

"Shut up," AJ grumbles with a smile. Before we took photos of all of us girls down by the gorgeous trellis Ryan built, someone noticed AJ missing. We all giggled and snapped photos of her sleeping in the rocking chair in Nolan's room, and have now teased her mercilessly since.

I follow my sister down the stairs and join the rest of my family in the living room. The door to the deck is open and soft music filters through the screen with the breeze. It's a gorgeous May day, one that couldn't be more perfect if it had been specially ordered from the heavens. A day that will see me professing my love to one man and ending with new titles of husband and wife.

Glancing around the room, my smile is instantaneous. All five of my sisters are there in matching dresses. My oldest niece is wearing an adorable little white dress, her own hair swept up in a braid and flowers. My dad is there too. His eyes are on mine, a soft, yet sad smile playing on his lips. There's one person missing from today, someone who should be here.

My mom.

I return his sad smile, knowing all too well what he's thinking. It was hard to plan this wedding without her. Like all of my sisters before me, I'm about to say "I do" without the woman who gave birth to me by my side. But I know she's here. I know she's looking down, with love and happiness in her green eyes.

With Josh.

They'll have a front row seat together.

"Ready?" Payton asks, handing me a white bouquet.

"Definitely," I reply, my heart starting to race.

I watch on as one by one, my sisters start to make their way out the door, down the stairs, and toward the beach. Payton first, followed by Jaime. Abby goes next, and then Lexi. AJ, my matron of honor, turns around and gives me a smile. I can see the emotions in it, feel them pouring from her. I feel the same way. It's that same mixture of jubilation and sorrow that I've felt all day. No, not because I'm not happy to be married, but because of the events that led to today.

She squeezes my bare hand with the one not holding her own bouquet before turning and walking out the door, leaving me alone in the house with my dad. He turns his full attention to me, his eyes shining brightly with unshed tears. Stepping forward, he places both hands on my upper arms and pulls me into a hug. "I've never been more proud to be your father than I am today," he whispers as he places a kiss on my forehead, just as he's done my entire life.

"Thank you, Daddy."

"She'd be so proud of you too. They both would." I don't have to ask who he's referring to. I already know.

A single tear slips from my eye as I nod my head in understanding.

"Nick is a lucky man, but he already knows that," he says with a soft smile. As he extends the crook of his arm toward me, he adds, "Shall we?"

Smiling up at him, I take his proffered arm. "Yes. Definitely."

My dad guides me toward the open door and into the sunlight. It's not too bright, thankfully, but it instantly warms my back. Carefully, we walk down the stairs and to the beach. Toward my future.

Family and friends all stand as I approach, but my eyes are riveted on one man standing at the front. Nick. My Nick. He's smiling widely, drinking in my appearance. As I approach, I notice how bright his eyes shine, unshed tears filling those perfect hazel eyes.

When we reach the front row of chairs, Dad and I stop. I glance to my right and smile at Nick's parents. His sister Natalie is there, too, while Stuart, Natalie's husband, stands up at the front by Nick's side.

Then I glance to my left and my heart starts to gallop in my chest. There stands Cindy, smiling brightly, unchecked tears streaming down her face. My own tears threaten to fall as I convey just how much her love and support has meant to me these last few years. We never say a word, but I know she understands when she gives me a head nod and reassuring grin.

My grandparents sit on the other side of her, their own happiness reflecting in their eyes. I can't help but wonder if Nick and I will have the kind of marriage they have. Maybe with a bit less over-sharing on the sexual details, but one where you adore the other person so much you can't help but tell them and show them every moment of every day.

I glance back at the second row, and even though I know they're there, my heart starts to pound when I see them. Josh's parents. John and Angie. Their own eyes are swimming with tears. My vision clouds as my eyes connect with Angie, who just gives me a knowing little grin.

Then, my eyes return to the row in front.

To the two empty chairs on the end.

To what those two chairs signify.

One for each of the two people who aren't here today.

My mom.

Josh.

A single corsage sits on the first chair, one that would have been worn by the mother of the bride.

A single red rose sits on the other, an ode to love that once flourished wildly in my heart. It's still there, that deep love, but now it occupies a bit less real estate than before.

Closing my eyes, I feel the breeze pick up in that moment, and I know he's here.

Just like he told me he'd be last night in my dream.

I offer a small smile and send up a silent thank you to the man who once loved me, and how he let me go. To the man who once held my heart in his hands, and then gingerly handed it over to another. To the man who will always watch over me, as I build and grow a life with someone else.

"Thank you, Josh," I whisper in the breeze, letting myself feel it as it washes over me

When I open my eyes and look forward, I'm staring at my future.

My forever.

Nick gives me a knowing, reassuring smile. He knew how hard it was on me, as this day on the calendar drew closer. I'll probably always be afraid that it could all be ripped away – that Nick could be stolen before our time was completed. That's why he reminds me to live for today. As Josh's mom once said, *'Tomorrow isn't a promise. Hold onto today with both hands.'*

"Who gives this woman to be married to this man?" the minister says from beneath the trellis.

"I do," my dad replies confidently, though I pick up the slight hint of emotion in his voice.

Turning to face the man who has been right by my side since day one, I offer my dad a bright smile. "Go," he whispers. "Live."

"I will. I promise," I reply right before he pulls me into his arms and kisses my forehead.

Then he lets go.

And I take a step in the opposite direction.

Toward Nick…

12

Nick

The moment I see her, I feel something so profound, so completely in my heart that it just makes everything right in the world.

It's her.

Stunning.

Breathtaking.

That's the only way to describe the incredible woman who now stands at my side.

I grab her hand as soon as she's within reach and bring it to my lips. There's a slight tremble, though I'm not sure if it's her hand or mine. Probably both. She looks up at me with so much excitement, so much happiness, that I don't pay any attention to the man standing in front of me, speaking.

I should probably pay attention, right?

But I can't.

I only see her.

My Meghan.

"Repeat after me."

And I do. I say the words, feeling them with every fiber of my being, as I vow to stand by her side, to love and protect her, till death do us part. It's an easy proclamation to make, since it's nothing but the truth. Her eyes fill with tears as she repeats the same vows as me, but she never wavers, never falters.

I know what is next.

When she suggested this part in the ceremony, I was completely one hundred percent behind her – or beside her.

Holding her hand tightly in mine, we walk over to the two empty chairs. Sobs echo around us as she reaches down and grabs the corsage and the single red rose. There's definitely a shake in her hand, but she remains steadfast and collected. She also squeezes my hand with everything she has.

Together, we walk to the shore. The waves are gentle as we approach. I help her hold her dress up as she kicks off the white flip-flops she insisted on wearing. I do the same, removing the tan slip-on boat-style shoes I'm wearing for my beachside wedding. I let go of her hand, only long enough to grab her dress. Side by side, we step into the cold water until it's lapping against our ankles. I reach for the corsage, the one made with the same white flowers as her bouquet, and together, we gently set it in the water. The corsage bobs up and down before slowly floating out into the Bay.

Then, she takes the rose. The single red rose that symbolizes love. Her love for a man who is no longer here. The one who held her hand and her soul before me. The one who died, leaving behind an amazing woman with the biggest heart, and I'm the lucky bastard who now holds that heart in my hands, cherishing and loving it with everything I have.

With trembling hands, we set that rose in the water and watch it slowly drift away.

The symbolism isn't lost on me, and I'm sure, not on Meghan either.

We stand together, our fingers entwined, as we watch both flowers float away. When I turn in her direction, she's not staring at the flowers in the water. She's looking at me. She's smiling with so much love and hope in her watery eyes that I almost drop to my knees right there in the water and thank the stars above for this gift I've been given.

Her love.

I switch hands, making sure that her dress doesn't fall into the surf (and let's not forget how much I want to rip that dress off her later), and guide her back to the sand. Our feet are wet, so we decide to forego shoes and simply walk back up to the trellis and finish this thing with bare feet. I love it, almost as much as I love her smile.

The minister says a few things, but I have no idea what. Her eyes sparkle like emeralds, and that's all I see. Her.

"You may kiss the bride," the man says with a knowing grin.

You don't have to tell me twice.

I pull her into my arms and steal our first official kiss as man and wife.

Wife.

She's mine.

Forever.

Epilogue

Meghan

It's a Summer sister tradition that on the first Saturday of each month, the six of us get together. We take turns picking the location or activity, anything from margaritas and a movie to wine and painting classes at the small gallery uptown. One thing, though, is as certain as the sun rising over the Chesapeake Bay every morning: there will be alcohol involved.

Always.

Tonight, the alcohol is flowing like water. We're celebrating. Everyone is dancing around AJ's backyard under the big white tent, carrying on and enjoying themselves. It makes me smile to see their happy faces, hear their jovial laughter. My family is the best, and I can't wait to share them with Nick.

"Still hanging in there?" AJ asks, her eyes starting to glaze over just a bit. Her son left just a few minutes ago, along with the rest of the kids. Dad and Cindy volunteered to take them all for the night, so we could all hang out and celebrate.

"Yes, though I have to admit, I'm a little anxious to get to the *later* part of the evening," I whisper to my sister.

She gives me a knowing grin. "He still hasn't told you where you're going?"

"Nope. Just to pack a bag for warmer weather," I reply excitedly. I knew he was surprising me with a honeymoon, but that's all I know. My new husband has kept his lips tightly sealed on this one.

AJ just grins like a loon. "You know, don't you?" I accuse, and know my assumption is correct the moment her eyes light up with laughter and guilt.

"Maybe," she draws out, her eyes glancing around the yard and landing on her husband. He looks like he wants to eat her alive right then and there, before excusing himself from the group he's talking to. He keeps his eyes on his wife as he slowly makes his way to the house, disappearing through their screened living room door.

"Will you excuse me?" she says, a subtle blush creeping up her neck.

"Where are you going?" I ask, though I already know the answer.

"To do laundry," she replies with a wink before practically sprinting up the stairs and into the house.

"Where is she going?" Payton asks as she approaches with Jaime.

"To do laundry," I state, taking another sip of my champagne.

Jaime snorts. "Laundry. That's code."

"Definitely," Payton agrees, looking over at her husband. He gives her a sexy little grin that makes me feel like I'm about to witness something that I can't unsee.

"Speaking of laundry," I mumble to Jaime, who starts laughing.

"Oh, she's going to be doing a load the moment she steps through the door," Jaime agrees with a laugh.

"Damn right, I am. No kids," Payton says, clinking her glass against Jaime's.

"No kids," Jaime mirrors, a knowing smile on her face.

Abby and Lexi join us at that moment. "Where's AJ?" Abby asks, glancing around the yard.

My two oldest sisters and I start to giggle. "Doing laundry," I answer.

"Is that what we're calling it now?" Lexi asks, her own laughter bubbling to the surface.

"Apparently," I reply with a shrug.

My sisters and I visit for a few minutes, but I have to admit, the weight of the day is starting to get to me. Even though I went with comfy flip-flops, my feet are getting tired and my muscles are starting to ache. The end of the night is drawing near, though I don't really want it to end.

My eyes immediately seek out the man who is now my husband. He's over with Rhenn, and the rest of the guys, all drinking something that is definitely not alcohol. Because our husbands are the best ever, they switched to non-alcoholic drinks a while ago so that everyone had a safe ride home.

His eyes meet mine from across the yard, and there's no missing the smile that graces his handsome face. Damn, I love that smile. It's warm and so full of love, and the best part is it's all for me. I return the knowing grin, watching as his eyes slowly peruse my body from head to toe. I almost feel naked, and for a moment, I wish I were. Though, this probably isn't the best time or place.

It's probably also not the best time to mention that I haven't had my period yet this month…

Nick turns and starts to make his way toward me, his eyes devouring me with a look of hunger and pure lust the entire way. My body starts to ignite in a slow burn, but with each step he takes toward me, it feels like he dumps a cup of gas on the blaze. By the time he reaches my side, I swear I'm going to die from desire, from wanting to be with him so badly.

"Hello, Mrs. Adams," he whispers in my ear as he wraps his big hand around my waist, pulling me into his side. I feel his erection immediately.

"Hello yourself, Mr Adams." It comes out all breathy.

"Oh, you are so gonna do it the moment you get on the plane," Lexi says.

"We're taking a plane?" I ask, my eyes bouncing between Nick and my sisters. I suspected, but this is the first piece of information that is confirmed.

Nick laughs. "We are."

"How long is the plane ride?" I ask, trying to swindle just a bit more info from him.

"Not telling," he replies, kissing the side of my head.

Soon, all of the husbands are joining our little circle, and the conversations turn dirty. Apparently, everyone is a bit excited to have a childless night at home. I lean into my husband's chest and listen to my sisters and brothers-in-law all laugh and tease each other. Rhenn is here too, along with my new sister-in-law and brother-in-law, Natalie and Stuart. They jump right in to the banter, as if they've been a Summer all along. It actually reminds me of my grandparents, who I haven't seen in a while…

When I glance around the yard, I finally spot them. Grandma is talking with a woman, and my attention is drawn to their exchange. The woman appears younger, probably about my dad's age, and she's twisting her hands together nervously in front of her. Grandma is the same ol' Grandma, her eyes and hands animated as she talks.

Then I notice my Grandpa. He's sitting at the table beside where they talk, gazing up at the woman with shock and awe in his eyes. Even from across the darkened yard, I can tell he's tense and maybe a bit apprehensive.

"Who's that?" I ask, knowing that this woman isn't anyone from my part of the guest list.

"Who?" Payton asks, glancing around the yard.

"The woman talking to Grandma," I reply, nodding that way with my chin.

Everyone turns and looks. "I'm not sure," Jaime says, which is quickly followed by similar replies from the rest of the group.

We all watch as Grandpa stands up and slowly makes his way to the woman. Before I know what hit me, he pulls her into his arms, hugging her with everything he has. The exchange brings tears to my eyes, even if I don't know what it's about. This woman means something to them, but what?

I grab my husband's hand and turn to my sisters. "I say we go find out…"

Another Epilogue

Emma

I knew this moment would be one of shock and happiness. The moment I found her, I knew that it would change the course of our lives forever.

"Mary Ann?" Orval asks, standing up and approaching the beautiful young woman at my side. My heart beats wildly in my chest. I've fretted a lot lately over how this reunion would play out. It's been years – too many years – and I knew it was time to change that. We're not getting any younger, you know.

"Hi, Orval," Mary Ann whispers, her voice tinged with nervousness.

"What are you doing here?" my husband asks.

"Emma invited me," she answers, nodding my way. I glance to my husband, hoping to convey how sorry I am for ambushing him this way, but needing him to know that I did it out of love.

"She did?" Orval says, a slight chuckle slipping from his lips. He doesn't say a word as he steps up to Mary Ann, his eyes locked on hers. They're identical in shape and color.

Before I can start to defend my actions, he pulls her into his arms and hugs her tightly. I don't miss the tears swimming in Mary Ann's eyes as she holds my husband closely, a soft smile gracing her lips. My own smile is instantaneous, and I finally know that I did a good thing.

I feel them all approach before I see them. My granddaughters. All of them, well, minus AJ who's probably inside pretending to do laundry with the sexy former ball player she's lucky enough to be married to.

"Hi," Meghan says, leading the pack.

"Good evening, Meggy Pie. It's a beautiful reception," I say to my granddaughter. her eyes bouncing back and forth between the three of us.

"Thank you," she replies politely.

"Oh, yes, congratulations to you," Mary Ann says to Meghan, who politely smiles, yet I can tell she's confused.

"Thank you," she says. "This is Nick, my husband."

"Nice to meet you," Mary Ann replies, suddenly nervous again as she takes in the many other pairs of eyes all looking at her.

"And you are?" Lexi hedges with a smile. Leave it to Lexi to not beat around the bush.

"Oh," Mary Ann chuckles uneasily. "I'm Mary Ann Grayson."

Before she can say anymore, my husband steps forward. "My sister."

Everyone stands perfectly still, shell-shocked and full of questions. "I invited her this evening," I confirm.

"You have a sister? How did we not know this?" Payton asks.

Orval chuckles, and motions to the table. "Why don't we sit down and I'll tell you a story."

They all follow suit, pull extra chairs from other tables until they're all seated around the table or near it. I take a seat beside my husband, his sister on his other side. Several sets of eager eyes all gaze up at us, anxious to hear how they have family that they never knew about.

"It all started more than sixty-five years ago. I was serving in the military, my sweet Emma waiting at home for my return. We had planned to get married the moment I came home, which was shortly after my twenty-first birthday." He gazes over at me, so much love still reflecting in his eyes that it still steals my breath. "We were married shortly after that, and started to plan the rest of our lives."

He takes a deep breath. "Unfortunately, a few weeks after our wedding, my mother became gravely ill. She had cancer." I can already tell how hard it is for him to say this. "Ovarian cancer," he whispers, his sadness washing over him like the waves off the Bay.

Several gasps can be heard at the table, and when I glance up, I see several tear-filled eyes gazing back at us. It's not lost on us that we lost both our daughter and Orval's mother to the same horrible disease.

"She died when I was twenty-four, mere weeks after sharing the news that she would be a grandmother."

I close my eyes, recalling how excited she was upon hearing our news. Even though we all knew – we knew in our hearts that she wouldn't live to see her grandchild brought into this world.

"My father, Samuel, didn't take her sickness so well. He became angry, and we fought. A lot. When my mother died, he drowned his sorrow the only way he knew how."

"My mother," Mary Ann says, her eyes full of sadness.

"My father moved on and married Mary Ann's mother a mere three months after my mother's death. I was still grieving, and the fact that he had so quickly replaced her with someone half his age, well, it angered me. So much so that I moved to a new town, me and my pregnant wife, to start over. My father moved his new family down to North Carolina."

Silence fills the yard. It's as if the party just sort of stops around us, even though I know it hasn't.

"I knew I had a big brother growing up, but that was about it. We were never close," Mary Ann adds.

"A twenty-five year age gap will do that," Lexi says.

"It will," Mary Ann agrees.

"So, you haven't seen each other in… how long?" Abby asks, her eyes full of unshed tears.

"Forty years," Orval replies sadly. "When my father died, his lawyer reached out to me. I saw Mary Ann and her mother, Phoebe, the day the will was read, but I didn't stick around long enough for anything else. My anger was all for him, yet I didn't know how to tell them. It wasn't their fault, yet I never told them that."

Mary Ann reaches over and grabs Orval's hand, giving it a gentle squeeze. When his eyes collide with hers, I feel the shift in the air. It's of forgiveness and hope. It's of family and togetherness.

"Wow, I have to say, I didn't see that one coming," Meghan says to herself aloud.

"What's going on?" AJ asks as she and Sawyer approach the table, her dress wrinkled and her hair thoroughly mused.

"Oh, you know. While you were sexing it up with the baseball god in your laundry room, we were here discovering that our Grandpa has a sister we didn't know about," Jaime tells her.

"What?" AJ hollers, dropping down to the empty seat beside me.

"It's true," Meghan replies with a laugh. "We might even have cousins."

"Cousins?" Abby asks, glancing around at her sisters.

"Yes, actually you do have cousins. I have four wonderful children who are your ages. I'd love to introduce you to them sometime," Mary Ann says with an easy smile.

"We'd love that," Meghan agrees.

"Then we'll make a plan," Mary Ann says to the group before her eyes land on her brother. "I hope it's okay if I come back sometime and bring my family."

I can see the tears filling his eyes. "I'd love that."

My heart pounds in my chest with elation. I wasn't sure how this evening would pan out, but I'm so glad I discovered that website. I'm happy I followed the lead that drove me straight to my husband's sister. And he responded the way I knew he would. Even though he was angry, I knew his anger was misplaced. I knew, if given the chance, he'd find happiness in knowing his sister.

He's a good man.

Mary Ann's phone starts to ring in her purse. "Oh, I'm so sorry. I thought I turned the ringer off before I got here," she says as she glances down at her phone. Her face becomes slightly concerned.

"Is everything all right?" Orval asks, looking down at the phone in her hand.

"I'm not sure," Mary Ann says uncertainly. "I have several missed calls from my daughter."

"You should call her back," her brother insists.

Mary Ann nods before placing the phone to her ear. She gets up from the table and takes a few steps away, giving herself a bit of privacy. My granddaughters all start to talk about this new development, anxious to meet their new family. It warms my heart that they will be able to connect with people who share their blood. Orval and I weren't able to have more children, so being able to give them this piece of family is important to me.

To us.

"Oh no! Are you okay?" Mary Ann exclaims, her hand covering her mouth as tears start to fall. She listens to whoever is on the other end of the line and starts to shake. Orval instantly gets up and goes to her, wrapping his arm around her back in a sign of support. "I'm on my way. I'll be there in a few hours," Mary Ann adds before disconnecting the phone call.

"What's wrong?" I ask, standing up. I feel everyone else stand up behind me.

"My home. My business. There's been a fire," she says, her voice cracking with emotion.

"A fire?" someone exclaims behind me.

"Yes, apparently, it started in my living quarters. My daughter, Marissa, was home, along with two couples who were guests, but they all made it out safely," she gasps, breathing hard and deeply. "I'm sorry, but I need to get going!" she adds, turning on her shaky legs and looking for her purse.

"You can't drive," I state.

"No, you can't," my husband agrees.

"Guests?" Payton asks.

"Yes, I own a bed and breakfast," Mary Ann announces, a few stray tears spilling from her eyes.

"We'll drive you," Orval proclaims.

"We can go too," Levi says, everyone nodding their heads vigorously.

"No, I couldn't ask that of you," Mary Ann insists.

"We're family," Jaime maintains, stepping forward and placing a hand on Mary Ann's forearm.

"Yes, family. Meghan and Nick, you two go on your honeymoon," I say. The moment Meghan starts to protest, I continue, "No, you two deserve this. You can't do anything now anyway." My newly married granddaughter gives me a look, conceding, but I can tell she doesn't like it. "Ryan, we could use your help on the contractor side in a few days," I add.

"Consider it done," Jaime's husband states.

"And we'll have to call an electrician. They are suspecting it was electrical," Mary Ann adds, her voice full of stress and worry.

"I can help," Rhenn says, stepping forward.

Nodding my head, I look at my family. "Rhenn, you and Ryan plan to come down tomorrow. Anyone else who wants to join them is welcome." I glance around at my family, my grandchildren, all so eager to help in someone's time of need.

Turning back to Orval, I grab his hand. "We're going now."

"Where?" Abby asks.

"To Rockland Falls..."

THE END

Join me in Rockland Falls, a small-town contemporary romance series.

Love and Pancakes, Rockland Falls, book 1

Love and Lingerie, Rockland Falls, book 2

Love and Landscape, Rockland Falls, book 3

Love and Neckties, Rockland Falls, book 4

About the Author

USA Today Bestselling Author Lacey Black is a Midwestern girl with a passion for reading, writing, and shopping. She carries her e-reader with her everywhere she goes so she never misses an opportunity to read a few pages. Always looking for a happily ever after, Lacey is passionate about contemporary romance novels and enjoys it further when you mix in a little suspense. She resides in a small town in Illinois with her husband and two children.

Website: laceyblackbooks.com

Email: laceyblackwrites@gmail.com

Sign up for my newsletter so you don't miss a single sale, reveal or release!

www.laceyblackbooks.com/newsletter

www.ingramcontent.com/pod-product-compliance
Lightning Source LLC
Chambersburg PA
CBHW071232170626
46809CB00008BA/3020